"Get in the ... s
shoving astronaut ...
"Did we get all ...

... Watts cried.

... Push off? Were they crazy? "We've
gotta make sure they got back!" he yelled, meaning the
other team.

"There's no time!" Sharp insisted.

"Where's A. J.?" Harry yelled.

"Get inside before this thing rips apart!" Sharp argued. He grabbed Harry. To Watts: "Shut the doors
and fire her up!"

Harry pulled away. "They're still out there!" he
yelled.

"It's them or all of us! This is an order!"
Watts screamed.

"We have to go now!" Tucker agreed.

"Full thrusters!" Sharp ordered.

And as the Freedom pulled away, the station
exploded into a fireball. Shrapnel narrowly missed the
shuttle as it sped off toward the moon.

"We've gotta ... this one over ... now!" A. J. ...
"That's what we ... better!" Harry replied.

ARMAGEDDON

ARMAGEDDON

a novel by M. C. Bolin

based on the screenplay by
Jonathan Hensleigh and the story
by **Jonathan Hensleigh** and **Robert Pool**

HYPERION

NEW YORK

ISBN 0-7868-8938-1

Designed by KimShala Wilson

FIRST EDITION

10 9 8 7 6 5 4 3 2 1

ARMAGEDDON

PROLOGUE

Sixty-five million years ago dinosaurs walked the face of a lush and fertile planet.

A complex, highly evolved ecosystem thrived. Then a piece of rock, only six miles wide, hurtling through space, altered the course of natural history forever.

An asteroid.

It struck the Earth with an impact equal to ten thousand nuclear weapons detonating simultaneously. The shock hurled a trillion tons of dirt and rock into the atmosphere.

A blanket of dust spread, blocking the sun for ten centuries.

It will happen again.

It's just a question of when.

CHAPTER ONE

65 MILLION YEARS LATER

Pete Shelby cursed under his breath—hoping the hundred-some-odd eavesdroppers couldn't hear. He wished he could reach up and wipe the sweat from his brow, but that was impossible in a space helmet.

He was screwing up here in his attempt to repair a satellite, and he was more than ready to hightail it back into the shuttle and burrow himself in the tiny scrap of security it offered. "Should've been a librarian like my mother," he muttered as he tried to gather his wits to continue. He could hear his heartbeat in his ears, could hear his puffy breathing, could damn near hear the sweat oozing from his pores.

"Houston, affirmative," he answered. "I'm gonna try it again."

Dan Truman leaned over the shoulder of his flight director, Walter Clark, watching the video.

"We've got the coupling up on the board now, Pete," Clark said. "We'll give you a heads-up from down here when it's in alignment."

Shelby's voice came through breathy and tense. "... Sounds good ... affirmative ..."

Truman grimaced. He didn't like the way Shelby sounded. He tapped Clark's shoulder and slipped into the seat when the flight director moved down a chair.

"Pete, this is Truman. We've got an eye on your meds down here. Let's try and relax a little. We've got plenty of time, buddy."

Floating high above Earth, with nothing but a damn clothesline between him and the depths of endless nothingness, Shelby thought, *Shit, man, easy for you to say!* But he forced himself to calm down as he struggled with the delicate instruments. It was like trying to do heart surgery with boxing gloves on.

"Okay, Houston," Shelby responded. "Advise."

Truman spoke slowly, calmly, distinctly. "Do not touch the gold plating. We don't want a power surge."

Shelby took a deep breath of canned air and ever so slowly moved the instrument into position. *Just take it slow and easy*, he told himself, *just like the bossman said. Slow ... and ...*

THUNK!

Shelby's last vision was of the reflection of Earth on his visor as it spiderwebbed into a dozen cracks.

Instantly the astronaut's blood boiled, steaming his soul off into those depths he'd so recently contemplated.

His corpse's sightless eyes never saw what hit him, but the impact spun his shoulder cam, which continued to hum, trying to record what was happening.

The space shuttle to which he'd been tethered was suddenly shredded by a hailstorm of thousands of tiny, speeding, meteoric pebbles. The NASA logo was destroyed, the skin of the mighty ship peeled down to the ribs.

The cockpit filled with a fireball.

And finally—the space shuttle exploded, spangling the dark void with some good old American Fourth of July fireworks.

Down on Earth, at Mission Control, the monitors went dead. Everyone froze, speechless, uncomprehending.

A horrible moment of silence enveloped the room—a silence filled with a million and one thoughts, none of them good.

And then a technician sprang to life and managed to croak into the silence: "We're down!"

That broke the standstill.

"Massive failure!" another tech reported. "We've lost—"

And suddenly his words were swallowed up in

the control center's familiar low-grade frenzy. Technicians dropped Styrofoam coffee cups and swung into seats. Hands flew across keyboards. Technical chatter washed over everything.

In the eye of the storm, Dan Truman stood rooted to the spot, beyond stunned, refusing to believe.

U.S. SPACE COMMAND, 4:49 A.M. EST

In a dark room filled with the most advanced machinery on the planet, a full battle staff ran to their posts. Tiny yellow blips filled several huge TV screens.

"Sector five-niner is reporting three—now five—eight—I repeat, eight unidentified tracks!"

"Watchdog!" another shouted. "I have four, now nine—make it eleven unknown—*shit!* I got tracks everywhere!"

From above on a catwalk a haggard-looking sector director yelled down: "It could be a surprise missile attack! Scramble the Eagles!"

OTIS AIR FORCE BASE, MASSACHUSETTS, 5:03 A.M. EST

Two dozen terrified pilots and crew got their butts in gear and scrambled onto the dark, frozen tarmac to their waiting F-15 Eagles.

_____

NATIONAL SECURITY COUNCIL SITUATION ROOM,
5:06 A.M.

The consoles lit up.

A young aide holding three phones spoke onto a secure line: "General Kimsey," he said nervously, "I have General Vladic from the Russian Air Defense Forces. He wants to know what we're doing."

_____

MISSION CONTROL, 5:09 A.M.

Dan Truman, in his late fifties, wiry, and tough as a two-dollar steak, paced through the jam-packed room, tossing out assignments. All hell was breaking lose, and he was in charge of figuring out how to fix it. "I want three groups. One—Internal malfunction. Hit the log tapes, start working back. Maybe it's a glitch. Two—I want NORAD, Space Command, and the Fiftieth Tactical comparing all space junk they track, in every orbit. Have 'em check then recheck, and then do it all over again. Three—Wild cards. Anything and everything."

He took a breath and glared around the room. "Let's move it!"

SEDONA, ARIZONA, 5:38 A.M.

Dottie woke up afraid to open her eyes before she felt the other side of the double bed.

The sheets were as cold as ice.

Muttering obscenities, she swung her stiff old legs out of bed and stuffed her cold feet in her furry slippers. She grabbed the plastic flashlight by the side of her bed, flicked it on, and stumbled through the cramped trailer. She paused only long enough to shine the flashlight across the trailer's tiny table, then marched out into the predawn darkness to the garage-sized, 1920s-vintage, amateur observatory out back.

"Karl!" she screamed into the night.

Inside the observatory she found him at last, her scrawny, good-for-nothing, eighty-year-old husband Karl, with his eye to the telescope.

"It's five-thirty in the goddamned morning!" she yelled. "Your Stouffer's pot pie's been on the table almost ten hours! I am sick and tired of pretty much everything in terms of you! I am *not* kidding anymore—I want a divorce!"

Karl kept his eye glued to the telescope's eyepiece.

"I thought we *were* divorced," he muttered.

"What was that?" Dottie shrieked.

But Karl's attention was on another fireball.

"This is something new," he said. "Dottie, go get my phone book."

"Excuse me!" Dottie exclaimed. "Am I wearing a sign that says Karl's Slave?"

"Go get my goddamned phone book!"

———————

WASHINGTON, D.C., PENNSYLVANIA AVENUE, 5:45 A.M.

In the back seat of an escorted military limousine, USAF Lieutenant General Kimsey, Chairman of the Joint Chiefs of Staff, turned to his deputy beside him.

"Space Command is reporting negative, that is, zero global launches," Army Lieutenant General Boffer reported. "It might be pieces of the shuttle re-entering the atmosphere."

"Yeah, and it might be Santa Claus!" Kimsey growled. "I want to get a definitive, reliable confirmation. Let's speed it up!"

———————

59TH STREET BRIDGE, MANHATTAN ISLAND, 6:00 A.M.

A bike messenger cruised through the stalled traffic, murmuring a rap song, swerving to the beat. He petted his bulldog in the bike's basket.

He parked and walked along the city street. It was so cool to be alive in the greatest city in the world—no, in the universe! The bulldog tugged at its leash, chewing up the sidewalk.

He shook his head at all the suits with their noses in the papers as usual. Hey, they were missing it—life was on Main Street, not Wall Street.

But as he passed a big electronics store he noticed a crowd gathering.

Maybe a game of three-card monte? he thought. *Nah, too many people for that.* He pressed himself into the crowd, squeezing into the gaps where normal-sized guys wouldn't fit.

"What's up?" he asked.

"Space shuttle," said the guy next to him. "Bam! It's gone. Vaporized."

Just then his bulldog lifted his leg and saluted a large boot—a boot connected to a huge guy from Samoa. The Samoan kicked the dog and the dog growled.

"Hey!" the little guy exclaimed. "Hey, you kicked my dog!"

"Little man!" the Samoan freaked. "Whatcha gonna do about it?"

"I'm gonna kick some Air Nike up your big—"

The last word was drowned out by a huge wrecking-ball noise overhead. The big-screen TV buzzed and blacked out.

The Samoan looked up into a shower of glass as a huge rock the size of a basketball drove him into the sidewalk and burst on the pavement. The plate-glass window exploded, TVs exploded, and people started screaming and yelling and running into the street, making the drivers honk their horns.

And then—

It was over. Steam hissed from a huge hole about ten feet wide.

The little guy huddled in a shell of the store, holding one end of his leash, which disappeared into the brand-new crater.

He crept to the edge and looked down. At the bottom of a forty-foot-deep crater hissed a sizzling, smoking, red-hot meteorite.

And there, dangling over the edge on the leash, was the bulldog. "Little Richard!" the little guy screamed. "Omigod! Call nine-one-one! Hang on!"

———

Throughout the city, traffic ground to a halt. A cabbie named Stu stuck his head out the window wondering what the hell was going on this time.

"What big problem?" asked the Asian tourist in his back seat.

"Could be anything," he said. "Shootin'. Stabbin'. Dead guy." He shrugged. "It's Friday, payday. Most probably a jumper."

Suddenly a projectile the size of a dump truck screamed through the sky and cut a straight line through three buildings in a row right before their eyes. More projectiles exploded in the intersection, wasting everything in line for the left turn.

Two cars tossed from a flipped parcel of pavement bounced down the block. The top five floors of one building broke off like the top layer of a wedding cake and shattered on the street below, smashing bricks, mortar, and gargoyles everywhere.

———————

MISSION CONTROL, 7:00 A.M.

"Space Command's screens are clearing," one tech called out.

"Sir," reported another, "it was a meteor shower in the northern hemisphere!"

"Stay focused," Truman ordered. "We need to map the trajectory *now*—"

"But, sir!" the tech said. "That could take over a week to—"

"Just find it," Truman ground out. "I want to know if the worst is over or on its way—"

"General Kimsey on line four," a guy across the room called out.

"Excellent." Truman punched the glowing button and picked up the phone. "Truman here."

General Kimsey was calling from the National Security Council room, surrounded by the Joint Chiefs. The TV news blared in the background. The President's chair was conspicuously empty.

"We've got hits from Finland to South Carolina," Kimsey barked. "We know they're not missiles, so what the hell is it?"

"Meteor shower," Truman explained. "That's what took out the shuttle."

"Well, I've got the President on Air Force One demanding answers," Kimsey said. "Is it over?"

"The sooner I get off the phone, the sooner I'll know. We'll call you back." He hung up without saying good-bye and turned back to the chaos.

———

Out in the corridors, Dr. Ronald Quincy dashed down the hall carrying stacks of paper.

"Quincy!" a tech called from a doorway. "I've got Karl on the phone from Sedona. Says he met you at a comet seminar. I think you should take this call."

Quincy gave Karl a minute and then passed him to Truman.

As Truman talked to Karl, the noise level in the room dropped. "...No, no, no, take your time, Karl," Truman said into the phone. "I'd rather have it right than fast." What he really wanted was both.

"No, no, you're definitely the first. ... Yes, we've all seen the news. ... I'm ready. Fire away." Truman gritted his teeth and ground his frown into a smile.

"Yes, I'm holding a pencil. Talk to me."

As he listened, a tech on a second line reported, "The FBI locked his location."

Clark listened in on another phone. "He saw an explosion in space. Been tracking a dim object for two weeks. It's a million to one, but this guy might have seen something."

"Karl," Truman said calmly, "I want you to stand by up there, okay? We're gonna send someone to get you. It's probably nothing, but for now I'm counting on you to keep this to yourself. Top secret, you understand?"

"Yes, sir," Karl said. "Sir, I'm retired Navy. I know what 'classified' means—but one more thing. The person who finds her gets to name her, is that right?"

"That's right," Truman replied, humoring the guy.

"I want to name her Dottie, after my wife," Karl said.

"That's sweet, Karl."

"Huh!" Karl shot back. "She's a vicious, life-sucking bitch from which there is no escape."

Hmm, appropriate, Truman thought.

———

Two STI—Space Tracking Institute—technicians manning the Hubble Space Telescope's control console rotated a camera lens on the satellite for a look at Karl's discovery.

"New Houston info—coordinates seven-one-two by three-four-five. Let's move fast on high-resolution imaging!"

Images from the Hubble arrived on a high-resolution printer. The technician grabbed four photos from the printer and swiped things off the console so they could lay them out and piece them together. Together they arranged the photos.

The two guys stared in awe at the image the composite revealed.

"Motherfu—"

———————

"Enough with this anomaly horseshit," the President growled over the phone. "What is this thing?"

"An asteroid, sir," Truman said.

"I'm staring at a laptop," the President replied. "How big are we talking?"

Truman glanced down the table. One of his Proportional Analysis guys spoke up. "Our best guess right now is ninety-six point five billion cubic kil—"

Truman waved his hands and mouthed, "Simple."

"Uh, it's the size of Texas, Mr. President."

"And we didn't see this coming?" the President asked.

"Our budget's basically gone, sir," Truman said. "You know, seven hundred thousand dollars doesn't go real far. We track three percent of the sky, and sir, excuse me, but it is one big-ass sky."

"What about this morning?" General Kimsey said. "How big were those?"

"Nothing," Truman said. "Pebbles. The size of basketballs and Volkswagens."

"Is this thing gonna hit us?" the President asked.

"We're efforting that as we speak—"

"What kind of damage are——?"

"Total," Truman said. "Sir, this is what we call a Global Killer. The end of mankind. Doesn't matter where it hits. Nothing would survive, not even bacteria."

"My God..." the President gasped. "What do we do?"

"Confirm our fears, review our options, and make the best choice we can."

Suddenly a door opened across the room. Truman and everybody else looked up and stared at the math guy who stood there holding a printout.

Shit, Truman thought. The guy didn't have to say a word. He knew it was bad.

The math guy cleared his throat and choked out, "We have eighteen days."

CHAPTER TWO

Harry S. Stamper pushed a tee into the grass, kissed the golf ball, then placed it gingerly into the tiny curve. It was a beautiful morning. What better way to start the day than to drive one into the sunshine? With patience and concentration, he eyed his target and lined up his shot. Exhale, relax, swing—THWACK!

Right on target.

THUNK!

The hard white ball banged the hull of the Greenpeace boat, rousing the protesters sleeping in the cockpit.

"Rise and shine!" Harry shouted gleefully as they began to return fire with angry words.

They continued to protest as he lined up the next shot from the deck of the oil rig. Behind him Charles "Chick" Chapple, a rugged man who had rough-necked with Stamper for twenty years, frowned. "That boat's a hundred yards too close. I'll call Massey—remember him? Navy buddy? He'll get those kids outta here nice and quick."

WHACK! Harry drove another ball into the hull of the ship. "Morning! How are ya? I know, we're the bad guys! Drillin' for oil's an evil thing! You know how much diesel that clunker boat of yours guzzles in an hour?"

Chick handed his boss a clipboard with a report. "I'm gonna call my friend. He's a riot. That bastard's so mean, even his own mother hates him."

"Nah, Greenpeace likes whales, I like whales. I just don't like when they park on my driving range." Harry quickly scanned the report. "Why was there drilling on Two?"

"Chewed a hundred eighty feet last night," Chick said.

"I shut it down," Harry said. "Who the hell ordered Two to drill?"

"I'll give you two guesses," Chick said. "But you're only gonna need one."

Harry's face flushed with anger, and he grit his teeth. With a growl he swung his golf club and hurled it into the ocean.

"Harry? That was my five iron," Chick pointed out.

Harry stomped through the rig, shouting, "A. J.! A. J.! Get your ass out here!"

A couple of roughnecks looked up from the pipe they were cutting. "What'd he do this time?" one chuckled as Harry marched into the superstructure.

Near the doorway, a mud logger geologist who

went by the name Rockhound sat in his boxers, a miner's helmet, and sneakers. In his gloved hands he was holding a big fish.

As Harry rushed past he called out, "Hey, Har! Check this out, man! Forty-three pounds of lean, mean, aquatic machine! Life in the goddamned food chain!"

"A. J.," Harry said. "Where is he?"

"Why?" Rockhound was suddenly serious now. "Hey, did we hit? Thank God! Are we done here?"

But Harry ignored him, hurrying on through.

" 'Cause you know me," he called after him, fish in hand. "I start fishin', it's the leading emotional indicator I'm getting a little rangy! Har—slow down!"

MISSION CONTROL CONFERENCE ROOM

All eyes were on Dan Truman as he read the mathematician's report. The numbers made it too certain—too *real*.

He looked around the room, hoping what he felt inside didn't show or spread to the others.

"All right, this is what we're going to do." His voice was quiet, but it carried well through the silent room. "I want every strategy we've got for Near Earth Object Collision. Every idea, every program, every sketch on every napkin and pizza box.

"For thirty years they've questioned the need for

NASA," he went on. "Today—we give them the answer."

A heartbeat later the room erupted into frantic activity. It was time to take everything they'd learned since first grade, every strategy they'd pulled off on the high school football field, every second of training they'd received at NASA—every prayer they could remember or make up—and pour it all into solving the biggest problem the world had ever faced.

CHAPTER THREE

Harry Stamper balled up all his fury and used it to slam open the door. As he filled the doorway, he peered into the tiny dark room and wanted to spit. Harry had those kind of eyes: hawk-like. He could see in the dark. He could see in your heart. Most of all, he could see through all fifty-seven varieties of bullshit. He should have known this was where he'd find the SOB. Still curled up in bed like an old dog. He took two long strides to the bed wedged into the darkest corner and kicked it. "Get up," he growled. "Before I drag you out."

A. J. sat up straight, trying to cover the fear he felt with the look of innocence he wished to convey. The result was bug-eyed. With his looks, A. J. could pose for cereal boxes—if he would only stop *posing*.

"Hey, okay," he said. "You're, uh . . . pissed. I get it—"

"No, you've seen me pissed," Harry snarled.

"This—you don't know what this is! I shut down Number Two! You knew that!"

"Huh?" A. J. froze with the look of a man on death row with the governor on line one. "Oh..." he said, realization dawning on him. "Oh! *That.*"

"Yeah, that!" Harry bellowed. "When you've got eight million of your cash on a contract—when it's your ass in the fire, if you don't hit at nineteen thousand feet, do whatever the hell you please. You don't ever disobey my orders!"

"Oh, man, yeah," A. J. said, sounding too happy for a man who was getting a dressing down from the boss. "Of course you're right. Lemme get dressed," he went on, pulling the covers up even higher. "I'll be up in two minutes."

Harry briefly wondered at A. J.'s odd modesty, but was too angry to consider it any further. "There are five words I need to hear from you. Right now. Five words."

A. J. frowned and counted as he talked. "I'm... sorry... Harry?" That was only three. "Very... sorry?"

"I'll never do it again!" Harry barked.

A. J. nodded like an eager puppy. "I won't, you know I won't. Who screwed up? Me. I blew it. Damn it, Harry, everything you're thinking, you're right." He chuckled like a cheap salesman who was trying to appease an irate customer. "I'll meet you at ops in five minutes. Okay?"

Harry's eyes narrowed as he stared A. J. squarely

in the eyes. Something stunk here. A. J. was just a little too apologetic for A. J.

Something was going on.

"I brought you on the job five years ago, A. J. And in all those five years, you've never apologized so quickly. This . . . this rush to contrition, I've gotta tell you, is making me nervous. Suspicious." He leaned in closer and peered into the guy's shifty eyes. "So tell me: What else did you do wrong?"

"Nothing, Har, I swear," A. J. promised with all his heart. "I'm just, you know, turning over a new leaf—"

Harry grunted and turned to leave.

"A-choo!" Light and girl-like.

Harry froze.

A. J. winced and sniffled and wiped his nose. He grinned.

Uh-oh.

Harry turned around, smiling like a crocodile. "What's that under the old leaf?" he said, and snapped the blanket off.

Lying there in slinky pajamas was a beautiful young woman, twenty-three, with tousled dark hair. The Greeks were still trying to perfect her statue.

Harry's jaw dropped. "Grace . . . ?"

"Harry . . . ?" she squeaked.

"I thought I told you to call me *Dad!*"

And just before Harry's angry red face turned a deeper shade, A. J. bolted from the room and slid down a seventy-foot cable.

Seconds later, Harry ripped a shotgun from its mount and chased after A. J.

"Harry? Harry!" A. J. cried. "Under the circumstances, being irrational is totally understand——"

BOOM!

It took A. J. a moment to ascertain that the shot had been fired into the sky and not into his gut——Christ, it was loud! "Holy shit, man!"

"I bailed you out of jail!" Harry cried, cocking the gun again. "I saved your life! I gave you a purpose! And this is how you repay me?"

"Will you *wait?*" A. J. shrieked. "Will you listen to me?"

But Harry was not the waiting kind.

A. J. scrambled up the derrick, above the deck and the water, climbing the metal rungs. Grace followed him with a sheet draped around her.

"Harry, stop it!" she shouted at her father. "You're being insane!"

"Sweetheart," he said without turning around, "go put some clothes on."

"You can't control my life, you know!"

"I know. Clothes. *Now.*"

Then he was after A. J. again.

"Look," A. J. said, panting hard as he painfully hurried up the metal rungs in his bare feet, "I'm only going to say this once: Put down that gun!"

BOOM!

A. J. nearly fainted as he felt the shots whiz past his underwear. Jeez, where the hell did the guy think he was aiming?

Harry cocked the gun again and aimed.

But then his view was blocked by a huge form. Jayotis "Bear" Kurleenbear, one of Harry's regulars, had earned the nickname not only as a shortened form of his surname, but also for his size.

"Why don't you put down the gun, boss?" he said quietly.

"You don't really want a piece of this, Bear. You know what I'm saying?"

Bear smiled. "Hell, yeah, I'm just trying to give my man a head start."

Harry shook his head and shoved past Bear. A. J. was still climbing for his life.

"You're still the same dumb-ass punk you always were," Harry shouted. "Only now you're just twice as old!"

"But, Harry!" A. J. pleaded, deciding it might work in his favor to be honest. "I love her!"

"*Way* wrong answer!" Harry fired again, this time grazing the pump jacks, sending a shower of sparks plummeting to the deck.

Just then Chick caught up with Harry. Chick—tousle-haired, easy-going, the voice of reason. "Harry, Christ, before you shoot the best man on your crew, get your ass on deck."

"I can't hear you," Harry said. "You're saying words, but I'm on a rampage—you've gotta move—" He pushed past Chick, going after A. J. with everything he had.

"We've gotta talk this over, man!" A. J. cried.

"That's what we're doing!" Harry replied.

BOOM!

The shot was too close and A. J. was moving too fast. He lost his footing and began to fall—

"No!" Grace screamed.

And then he just snagged a cable. He used it to pull himself to safety as Harry aimed at him.

I wouldn't really shoot the kid, Harry thought as he aimed at A. J. Then he thought of that punk in bed with his daughter—right here under her father's nose!

Justifiable homicide? He was a cinch for acquittal if there were any fathers on the jury. . . .

AHHHHNNNNNNNNNNNNNNNN!

An air-horn blast stopped them all in their tracks. It never blasted unless something important was going on. Harry glanced down on deck to see Rockhound waving at them.

"Pucker up!" Rockhound hissed up. "We've got clients incoming!"

The crew immediately turned their eyes across the water where a huge liner had appeared on the horizon.

Harry lowered his gun. Business came first. The family squabble would have to wait.

———————

At Mission Control, the presentation table was littered with books, reports, sketches, scale models— dozens of half-baked, theoretical proposals propped up with *ifs, ands,* or *buts.*

The young planner's hands shook as he tried to explain his idea. "Uh, we, uh, back in 1974, the idea—the possibility that an asteroid—you could say, meteor . . . though, technically a meteor is just a—"

Truman rolled his eyes. Fuck this crap. They'd all be infinitesimally small particles of antimatter before this kid got to the point. "I need someone who's had less caffeine this morning," he snapped. "Grunberg, translate."

"Our first feasibility plan was to use a spread-focus laser generator to heat the object to the point of fracture—"

"That's shooting a BB gun at a freight train," Truman interrupted impatiently. "Alexander, whatcha got?"

"What about electrostatic repulsion?" Alexander asked.

"What about it?" Truman snorted. "We've got two and a half weeks. We can't bank on ER in this scenario. Waisler. Go."

Waisler held up a schematic drawing, pointing to various dotted lines as he explained, "We've got the design for sending a craft to the object and hoisting solar sails to gently redirect its trajectory."

"Nice. Creative."

Waisler's face fell. "You don't like this idea."

Truman didn't blink. "No. What else have we got, people?" He glanced irritably at the clock—the official NASA stopwatch. The clock expressed time in digital numbers down to the thousandth of a second. Time to global impact: 18 days. 431:15:18:014.

"Time's a luxury we don't have."

———————

Back on the oil rig, Harry's ragtag crew of roughnecks assembled on the deck, trying to present a professional appearance as they watched three Hong Kong executives prepare to make their way up the gangplank from their sleek yacht to Harry's muddy rig.

Grace stood at her father's side, now completely dressed, presenting the picture of professionalism. A still-nervous A. J. stood off to the side next to Bear.

But Grace's cool demeanor was a business facade, which barely covered the anger inside.

"I understand that you're handicapped by a natural immaturity, Harry—"

"Dad. Call me Da—"

"I'm not gonna end up like you—alone, obsessed with my work, without a life partner...."

"I've got partners," Harry said, hurt. "Bear's been with me ten years, Chick's going on twenty—"

"A. J.'s *my* choice, Harry. I chose him. I want you to respect that."

"He's the only one in your age bracket, honey!" Harry protested, keeping his eye on the advancing Asians. "That's not a choice—it's a lack of options."

Grace rolled her eyes. "Okay. Since *you're* the great expert on the subject of boys and girls together," she said, her voice dripping with sarcasm, "tell me: Where's my mother again?"

"Do *not* start with that—"

"Oh, that's right," Grace said, pretending to remember, enjoying it now, knowing she was getting to him. "Nobody knows. When she bailed, she forgot to leave us a forwarding address."

"Grace," Chick interrupted quietly, "I think you're crossing the line."

Grace ignored the older man and went on, enjoying her attack. "She was a good choice, Harry. You're a relationship expert."

"Hey, that's your mother you're talking about!" Harry protested.

Grace shook her head. "What do you want from me, Harry? I can't be the cute, neutered, little mascot all my life—"

"I want you on a crewboat back to the mainland and back in the office by Monday."

"Really. Then I quit."

Harry shook his head. He'd spoiled the girl, he told himself. Let her get too independent. Well, he'd show her who was in charge. She could take orders as well as any personnel on the rig. "You're not gonna quit," her father ordered. "And you're not gonna start seeing A. J., and we're not gonna have this conversation. Understood?"

Harry wondered why she was laughing. "What?"

Grace barely smothered her laughter to step forward and greet their clients from Hong Kong, who were instantly charmed by her perfectly accented, fluent Cantonese.

Harry, of course, had no idea what the fuck they were all talking about, but he nodded and grinned and bowed, and in between phrases of Cantonese, his daughter, still smiling at her clients, continued their argument.

"I've been dating A. J. for six months!"

Harry was thankful his clients didn't understand a word of the sudden epithets that flew from his lips at the news.

Then Grace began to lead their clients on a grand tour of the ship.

Harry hurried to keep up. "Have I once—ever—prevented you from doing anything?"

"What about having a life?" Grace said in an aside as she smiled at her clients. "You know I just learned that most children don't live off the coast of eighteen countries before they're nine. I didn't know that, did you?"

"So you're worldly," Harry said. "You're welcome. You speak five languages because of me! I think that merits a *merci*, a *grazie* . . ."

"And most girls don't borrow a razor to shave their legs for the first time from a three-hundred-pound man named Bear. First time I got my period, Harry? Rockhound had to take me into Taipei for Tampax. And then he had to show me how to use them—"

Harry turned his hard gaze on Rockhound, who

giggled nervously. "I had to *tell* her how to use 'em, Harry. Not show her...."

"I was playing with titanium depth gauges when I should have been playing with dolls," Grace ranted on. "I learned about the birds and the bees from Max's tattoos. And I wore my first dress to go to a driller named Rocky the Rhino's funeral. I celebrated my thirteenth birthday in a brothel in Managua with Chick, Max, and eleven hookers named Rosa...."

"Ah, Rosa," Max remembered. "Every one of 'em...."

"I was raised on roughnecks, Harry," Grace went on. "By you. And then you get all shocked and shaken when I fall in love with one?"

Harry stared back at her, devastated.

Grace faced him, hands on hips. "I grew up, Harry. Maybe you blinked, maybe you missed it. But I don't play with titanium depth gauges anymore."

Harry opened his mouth to respond when suddenly a *thump-thump* noise distracted him. Around them pipes were vibrating. He quickly checked the pressure gauge. Son of a bitch, it was peaking! The needle dropped, then jumped——once, twice——

Harry's eyes popped open as he sprinted away.

Grace watched her father in total confusion.

A. J. joined Harry with a triumphant smile.

"Is that Number Two?" Harry shrieked.

"Gotcha, man!" A. J. answered proudly. "We hit! I told you!"

"I closed it down for a reason, you idiot!" he

shouted. "Two's relief valve is fried open!" To Grace, he shouted, "Get those people out of here!"

Ka-whoosh! Oil, pipe, mud—all of it rocketed into the sky.

"Chick!" Harry shouted. "Turn the table out— move! Bear, Max—swing those back-flanges in! Go! Go! Go!"

A. J. charged after Harry. Grace pulled their confused clients into hiding just as—

WHAM! Oil ruptured a valve and created a black fountain on the platform. Chick and his team pulled cable and equipment as fast as they could to stop the flow, putting on a good show for the customers.

Harry made the best of it. He smiled brightly through the oil on his face and explained:

"It's only a test, gentlemen. Emergency management drill—you can never be too prepared!"

———

In Houston, the emergency couldn't have been more real.

There was no time to be exhausted, Truman told himself as he rubbed his forehead and sat down in another meeting—this one which included General Kimsey.

"With the proximity of the asteroid and no prep time, none of our primary plans can work."

"Why don't we just send up a hundred and fifty

warheads and blow that rock apart?" General Kimsey asked.

"Good question," said a man seated in a chair across the table. "Bad idea."

Kimsey glared at the guy. "Was I talking to you?

"This is Dr. Ronald Quincy from Research," Truman explained to the general. "Pretty much the smartest man on the planet. You might want to listen to him."

Quincy leaned forward as he explained to the general. "Consider your target. Her composition, her dimension, her velocity. You could hit her with all the nukes you want, and she'd just smile at you."

"You should know," Kimsey said, "that the President's science advisers suggest a nuclear blast could change the asteroid's trajectory."

"I know those advisers," Quincy shot back. "We all went to M.I.T., and I can tell you, in a situation like this, you do not want to listen to a man who got a C-minus in Astrophysics. His advisers are wrong."

"Hitting the rock from the outside won't do the job," Truman added.

"What do you mean, the *outside?*"

"You set a firecracker off in your open palm, you get a burn," Truman explained. "But close your fist and light that fuse—and your wife's gonna be opening the ketchup bottle for the rest of your life."

"You're suggesting we nuke the thing from inside?" Kimsey exclaimed. "How?"

"We drill," Truman said matter-of-factly. "We bring in the world's best deep-core driller."

The world's best deep-core driller was at that very moment dealing with a sticky situation of his own. The oil fountain on the rig had coated the platform and everything and everyone on it, making the "drill" a special challenge. Pipes slid and rolled in the slick under Harry as he raced to get to the giant valve wheel.

He struggled to close it, but it wouldn't budge. It was too slick, and Harry was being blinded by the oil anyway.

It looked hopeless until A. J. charged into the mess and pushed his way in beside Harry. Together, muscles groaning, they managed to turn the wheel. Slowly, slowly they stemmed the flow.

And then they took a break and sat down in the black pool. A. J. smiled at Harry, his teeth the only spot of white in sight.

"Don't smile at me," Harry said. Slipping in the oil a little, he struggled to his feet and walked off.

Then he froze when he saw Grace come out of hiding with the Hong Kong clients—all covered in oil. Not good, Harry thought. The men, their suits and ties—even their yacht was oily black.

Only their smiles were not oily black.

"Thumb high, Harry!" one of the men exclaimed in broken English. "You a man! Many thumb!"

With a shaky smile, Harry managed to raise his thumb and duplicate the man's gesture. Then he turned to Chick, who stood high on the bridge. "Everyone all right? Are we holding?"

"We're great, Harry," Chick called down. "PPI's at eighteen hundred solid!"

Harry nearly bit his tongue in two when he suddenly felt someone slap him hard on the back. Growling, he turned to find A. J. at his side.

"You know, you should tell me next time we got an open blow-out valve, all ri——?"

WHAM!

A. J. hit the deck before the pain from Harry's fist smashing into his face reached his brain. Grace gasped and hurried across the platform toward the men.

"I just made this hit, Harry!" A. J. said, incredulous.

"*Getting lucky doesn't mean you're any good,*" Harry ground out. "*Someone could've died today!*"

A. J. felt his jaw and struggled to his feet just as Grace rushed to his side. "I'm lucky *and* I'm good," he shot back.

"Oh, yeah?" Harry shoved him. "This lucky?" He shoved him again. "Or good?"

WHOK-WHOK-WHOK.

Everyone—including the Asians—looked up at the sound of helicopter rotors. Harry squinted into the morning sun and frowned in question. A Seahawk helicopter, and it wasn't just passing over. The damned thing was getting ready to land—right on the deck of his oil rig!

The crew fell into a lazy formation around the platform as the helicopter set down. Six big Marines debarked onto the deck. After them came a decorated older officer. Harry took him for an admiral.

"Who's Harry Stamper?" the man called out.

Harry shook his head in disbelief. "And it's not even nine o'clock yet," he muttered. Then, raising his voice, he called out, "Over here!"

The soldier came to him, stepping gingerly across the oil slick. "We need to talk," he said. "Privately."

Harry led him inside.

"Mr. Stamper, I'm Admiral Kelso, Commander of the Pacific Fleet. I've been sent here by the Secretary of Defense on direct orders from the President of the United States. This is a matter of urgent national security. I need you to get on this chopper right now, no questions asked. Reassure your men that you're leaving voluntarily."

Harry cocked his head sideways and grinned at the big soldier. "Did Crazy Willy put you up to this?"

"I'm afraid I don't know any Crazy Willy," Admiral Kelso said gruffly. "Sir, I'm dead serious about this."

Harry grinned back, waiting for the punch line. But as he stared into the admiral's reflective sunglasses, it suddenly dawned on him that this was for real. Before he could think of what to say, Rockhound stumbled over.

"Listen, I swear to God she never told me her age," he was mumbling nervously, "so I assumed she was at least——"

"No," Harry interrupted him. "This is about me."

"Oh. Oops! Forget it...." Rockhound said, slinking off.

Harry made a decision in his usual way: quickly. He glanced over at Grace and A. J., who were heavy into their own conversation.

"I'll go with you," Harry said, so only Kelso could hear, "on one condition...."

――――― ―――――

Grace and A. J., in the midst of their own drama, were unaware of the four Marines bearing down on them.

"I thought it went pretty well," A. J. said. "Considering..."

"Considering what?" Grace said, offering him a little of the same pepper that she'd dashed on her father. "That he's in some kind of wigged-out denial about me? That he thinks you're his son? In his mind we've *trespassed*, A. J.——"

"Honey, we should have found a way to tell him, that's all."

"Now you're taking his side?" she exclaimed. "The man just punched you——"

Her words broke off as a tall wall of Marine

stepped between them. "Miss, you're requested on board. National security."

Stunned, Grace glared at him. "National security—and you want *me*?"

Grace and A. J. shared a look of confusion just before two Marines appeared on either side of A. J. and lifted him up under the arms.

Grace began to yell out a protest just as the other two Marines lifted her into the air.

Already seated in the chopper, still covered with oil, Harry watched with a huge smile on his face as Grace was "escorted" into the helicopter.

"Chick!" Harry shouted over the beating of the chopper's blades. "You're in charge! Get 'em home today! Mr. Fong—you look great in black!"

JOHNSON SPACE CENTER

Harry and Grace had been on a long, unplanned trip halfway around the world, and they were tense, tired, and confused as they were ushered into a meeting room at the nation's space headquarters. So far nobody had explained a damn thing about what was going on.

Dan Truman held out his hand. "Mr. Stamper. Ms. Stamper. I'm Dan Truman. I'm the executive director here. On behalf of everyone, please accept my apolo——"

"No," Harry interrupted. "No more apologies.

We've had eighteen solid hours of apologies. Apologies on three helicopters, one aircraft carrier, and two military jets. We've been apologized to in half a dozen time zones, so please, for Chrissake, spit it out already!"

For a moment there was silence as the two men stood eye to eye, sizing each other up. Then Truman cut a look at Grace.

"There isn't a thing in this world I keep from my daughter," Harry said, "so whether you tell her or I tell her, she's gonna find out. Your choice."

Truman nodded and led them upstairs to a large conference room. He lowered the lights and began to show them the hastily thrown together presentation that would explain their problem.

"... A rogue comet hit an asteroid belt," Truman was saying, "sending shrapnel right for us. We're in a shooting gallery for the next two and a half weeks. Even if this asteroid hits water, it's still hitting land. It'll flash-boil millions of gallons of sea water and slam into ocean bedrock. A Pacific impact and a tidal wave three miles high travels a thousand miles an hour, covering California, washing up in Denver. Japan, gone. Australia, gone. Half the world's population gets incinerated by the heat blasts, the rest freeze to death by nuclear winter."

There was complete, dead, grim silence as the lights slowly came back up again. Grace reached for her father's hand, and Harry held it tight. The two of them sat without speaking, numb from shock.

"This is unreal," Harry breathed at last.

"Mr. Stamper," Truman said, "this is as real as it gets." He nodded at two of his techs, who opened the curtains along one of the room's walls, revealing windows that looked down on a very hectic mission control.

"It's coming," Truman assured them. "Right now. At twenty-two thousand miles an hour, right for us. And none of us—anyone, anywhere—can hide from it."

Harry swallowed. "I take it . . . you're not alerting everyone like this."

"No one knows," Truman said firmly. "And that's how it stays. For the next ten days, only nine telescopes in the world can spot the asteroid, and we can control eight of them. The President's classified this information as confidential. Those were the forms you signed." He handed Harry a notebook. "Study from eighty-seven. If news like this broke, there'd be an overnight breakdown of basic social services worldwide. Rioting. Mass religious hysteria. Instant erosion of central authority. That thing reads like Cliff Notes to the worst parts of the Bible."

Harry shook his head in amazement. Now for the big question. "So there are six billion people on the planet. And you call me. Why?"

Truman led them out into the hallway, accompanied by Quincy and a small military escort. "We want to land on the asteroid, drill a hole, drop in some nukes, take off, and detonate. Except we have an equipment problem."

Two armed guards opened some doors, and they stepped into the R & D hangar.

"The drilling unit is part of a lunar project we've been working on for the past three years," Quincy informed them. "The recent discovery of water on the moon wa——"

Harry gasped. The room was filled with technicians hovering around a huge gurney. Stretched across it was a large robotic drilling arm—complex machinery, gears, and Teflon cables. Harry's jaw tightened as he circled the equipment. *What the hell——?* He couldn't believe what he was looking at. This couldn't be!

"Uh," Quincy said nervously, "you might recognize the rig——"

"It's tough not to recognize something you spent five years designing," Harry said incredulously. It was *his* rig—all his, made of his sweat and tears and dreams. Except here it was, in the flesh, brought to life by NASA technicians. It was like finding your wife in bed with another man.

"Yes," Quincy said. "We were planning on sending this to the moon and——"

"What, you got a key to the Patent Office?" Harry exclaimed.

Truman shrugged. "Basically."

"I got dragged into this because you stole from me?" Harry nearly shrieked. "And by the way, did a shit job of putting it together?"

"So what's wrong with it?" Truman asked. "You said we'd done a bad job putting it together."

"No, no, I said *shit* job," Harry corrected the man. "First of all, you've got the return system backwards. I'll take a guess—you're tearing up rotors and can't figure out why."

"Yes, that's right. . . ." Quincy said, amazed.

"Well, the cams are all wrong, Mr. Wizard," Harry said. "The low cable, the way it's jammed in there? Wrong. And what's this? Aluminum?"

"Ceramic-titanium," Quincy said.

"If you're gonna steal a blueprint," Harry sneered, "at least read the materials list. How do you short-hitch ceramics?"

"What if the bit starts binding?" Grace added. "There's no flexibility. That's what he means."

"Who's been operating this thing?" Harry asked.

Truman beckoned across the room and eight NASA mission specialists started walking toward them.

Harry made a face. "What's this?"

"We've had them training for eight months," Quincy said.

For the first time in two days a smile crossed Harry's face. "Eight whole months? Gosh . . ."

"We need you to modify the equipment and help train this team," Truman said seriously.

"Team?" Harry scoffed. "That's not a team. It's a Dungeons and Dragons convention." He glanced over at this so-called team. *Okay, let's see if these nerds are up for a pop quiz!* "Here's one for you! You hit a gas pocket at three hundred feet. Your crown block's frozen, the Kelly's starting to kick. You've got flow pressure backwashing, and the valve swing's just broken off in your roughneck's hand. What do you need to know?" The weasely-looking techies stared at one another. *Okay, guys, five seconds . . .* "Quick!" he shouted. "Do you pull pipe, speed up, slow down, or run like hell?" The techies stared at Harry as he grinned and counted, *one, two, three . . .* "Time's up. The rig blew. We all die."

The room fell silent. Everyone stopped working and stared at Harry. Then at Truman.

"Look," Harry said, "I'm a third-generation driller. I drew my first paycheck when I was twelve years old. It took me thirty-two years, every day—every friggin' minute—to learn what I know. And I'm still learning. Some guy with one hand in a bar told you about a piece of equipment you've gotta watch out for, that kinda thing. Might not look like it, but drillin' holes is an art. If you don't know your crew as well as you know yourself, you're dead. I'm the best because I work with the best. In seventeen days I couldn't teach these Trekkies any more about drilling than you could teach me to fly a damn spaceship."

The eyes of Harry Stamper and Dan Truman locked across the room. Each man's mind was racing.

At last Truman spoke. "You got any other ideas?"

"All they have to do is drill?" Harry asked.

"That's it."

"No spacewalking?" Harry asked. "No crazy astronaut stuff?"

Truman nodded slowly. "Just drill."

Suddenly Grace interjected, "Uh, yeah, *just drill.* On an asteroid flying twenty-two thousand miles an hour!"

"Drop the bomb, take off, and detonate——"

"That's the plan," Truman said.

"And if it doesn't work, we all die anyway."

"All of us. Everywhere."

"How many men?" Harry asked.

Truman shrugged, his face intent, now that he felt a nibble on his line. "Two teams, you tell me—there are two shuttles going up."

"I'll need eight men per crew——"

"We've only got room for four."

"Then that'll have to do."

Grace's face was livid. This was insane! "This is bullshit, Harry. You know that, right? You don't have to do this!"

There was a long pause as Harry glanced first at Truman, then at his daughter.

"Yeah, I do. I don't trust anyone else."

CHAPTER FOUR

"As soon as they're off the rig, the guys scatter—make up for lost time," Harry said. "I don't know how you're gonna find 'em, but I'm taking Bear."

On a lonely ribbon of highway in some forgotten scrap of American countryside, a Harley roared down the blacktop like a wild animal released from a cage. Bear Kurleenbear was doing what he loved best: riding with just the horizon on his mind, with rarely another human being in sight.

But then Bear's eyes caught movement in his rear-view mirror. Shit. There, materializing through the wavering lines of the heat rising from the road, was another human being in sight, the worst kind—the kind that liked to drive around in cop cars. This one had his lights flashing, with Bear the only prey in sight.

And then, as Bear watched, another black-and-white crested the hill. Damn! Something was up, and these dudes meant business.

Bear grabbed the left clutch in his meaty hand and kicked into high gear with his left foot. The wind snatched the words from his mouth as he shot forward, bellowing: "Come 'n' get me, bitch!"

———————

Harry and Grace flipped through Stamper Oil personnel files—with a team of FBI agents hanging on every word.

"Ox ... Cobb ... they're thick in the head," Grace said. "You need smart. That's Max."

———————

Max Lennert was a big wall of a man, with plenty of canvas for the illustrious tattoos he loved to collect all over his body. In fact, he was enjoying his time off by having another one engraved on his massive arm, a special one this time, to commemorate a special person in his life.

Max lowered his *Wall Street Journal* as his sweet old momma came in carrying a box of doughnuts. "Like it, Momma?" he asked hopefully.

His momma peered over the shoulder of the tattoo artist as he put the finishing touches on his last work of art. "LOVIN' MOMMA," it read. Momma smiled.

"Did you get me one of those yellow-jelly bear claws?" Max asked her, his voice like an eager little boy's as he reached for the cardboard box.

"Maxie," his momma whispered, nodding her poor head in the direction of the front door, "I think you're in trouble with the law again...."

Max flinched as he saw two FBI men walk in the door.

———————

"Two geologists. Gimme Hound," Harry said without a moment's thought.

———————

Rockhound was almost as drunk as the blond bimbo draped onto the bar and bar stool beside him in the small drinking hole in the French Quarter of New Orleans. In one hand he held the dame's left hand, which sported a huge, sparkly ring. In the other he held his loupe, trying to examine the stone.

"Isn't it easier if I take it off?" the blond slurred.

"Hey, don' rush me," Rockhound replied with a lopsided grin that he intended as a cosmopolitan leer. "We got plenty of time for that later." He hiccuped. "Just kidding. Uh, so what'd he tell you he spent on this, anyway?"

"It's over two carats," she said proudly.

"Yeah, well, size isn't everything. Although in my case, it's something." He looked at her, trying to tell if she was smiling. "Okay, so the ring . . . How should I put this? This diamond isn't—"

The blond frowned in disappointment. "Isn't two carats?"

Darn, she was awful pretty, and he sure hated to break her heart, but then, hey, if she burst into tears or something over the jerk . . . Who just happened to be sitting right next to her with a shoulder just waiting to be cried on? "It isn't a diamond."

Sure enough, her face crumpled like aluminum foil. If she wasn't in his arms within five minutes, rubbing those beautiful gems of hers up against his chest . . .

Suddenly Rockhound managed to focus his eyes on some other striking figures that now loomed over him—two men in suits. Uh-oh, could this be her fiancé and his bodyguard or something? He leaned across the bar and whispered rather loudly, "Are these your friends?"

The blond shook her head; she was as oblivious as he was.

"Sir," one of the men said in an official-sounding voice, "we have a national security matter."

———   ———

"Second geologist?" Harry thought a split second. "Oscar's the man."

"Yeah," Grace agreed. "If they can find him . . ."

On the great southwestern plains of America, a young man galloped across the desert on a gray stallion into the setting sun, like something out of an old movie.

Except for the two helicopters skimming the ground behind him...

"Engineers," Grace said. "You'll need your right-hand man. . . ."

Harry nodded. "Chick, obviously."

Chick Chapple had come to Las Vegas hoping to turn his latest paycheck into a retirement fund. But right now, leaning over the craps table, rattling the dice, it was looking more like his funeral. He summoned some of the guts it took to work for Harry Stamper and flung the dice across the table.

Hot damn!

Seven!

Whooping in delight, Chick reached across the table and scooped the money toward him like a man embracing his lover. Only one thing ruined the mood.

Two stiff-looking suits standing just a little too close on either side of him.

"Mr. Charles Chapple?" one guy asked.

"Before I answer that," Chick said suspiciously, "let me ask you this: Has there ever been a situation where someone's been approached by two men in identical suits and it's been good news?"

———————

"Engineer number two..."

"How'd you leave it with Freddy Noonan?" Grace asked.

"I paid the hospital bill," Harry said. "He paid for the holes in the wall."

———————

In the bright morning light in the alleyway behind a bar, Freddy Noonan was hanging his latest piece of work on the chipped brick wall. As the jerk gasped for a break, Noonan browbeat the guy in his thick Aussie accent: "The mates I collect for'll gladly accept your cold dead ass instead of payment—you make the call. I'm easy."

But then Noonan's ears picked up the sound of a footstep, and he released his choke hold on the guy and whirled around. Two huge guys in suits had somehow snuck up on him.

"Ladies," Noonan said with a nod, "whatever it is, I probably did it."

Behind him, his "client" was recovering and, assuming he'd been saved by somebody, starting mumbling tough stuff: "Weasel-punk, no-brains foreigner—"

WHAM!

Noonan reeled around and cold-cocked the guy, hard, and the weasel bit the ground.

———

And now they came to the inevitable. Through some unspoken agreement, father and daughter had been putting one choice off till last.

"You'll still need another tool pusher," Grace said at last, conscious of the FBI gúys eavesdropping. "Everett's probably in Houston right now.... How about Bennie? He's good."

Harry sighed and looked away. There was one name on both minds. Or rather, two initials. Who was going to speak it first—him or her?

Grace shifted in her seat. "You don't want A. J., right? He's too reckless. He's cocky ... dangerous. And fired, so—"

"I need him," Harry said reluctantly.

"I thought you said you couldn't trust him—"

"I thought *you* said I *could.*" Harry sighed again and looked his daughter in the eye. "That drill's my design. No one knows her like me. Except A. J."

Grace struggled to come up with some kind of argument, something to keep A. J.'s feet—and other desirable parts—on the ground. But she couldn't.

Her dad was right. And hey, what good was having A. J. on Earth if...?

She shrugged. A. J. was on the team.

———— ————

Once Harry Stamper had never turned away from a job, no matter how tough, no matter how disgusting. But it took most of his strength to face the undesirable task that lay before him. He'd come to beg A. J.

A. J. poked his head under the hood of his old sixties muscle car with a wiseass grin on his face. "So what you're basically saying here," he said, loving the hell out of the situation, "lemme just get this straight—is that there's a job Mr. Stud Harry Stamper can't handle by himself."

Harry tasted blood from biting his tongue so hard. He cleared his throat. "Yeah...more or less."

"Well, I don't get it," A. J. said. "Is it more or is it less?"

Harry stared into the kid's eyes with a look that could boil water. "You and I have a real problem."

"Harry, there are five words I wanna hear right now," A. J. said, enjoying throwing Harry's own words back into his face. " 'A. J., I need you, man'— No!—'A. J., you're the best...ever.' " A. J. chuckled. "How about four words: 'A. J., I love you.' "

"I'm not here to boost your ego," Harry ground out. "You should know there's not a job on this planet I'd want you to work on. I mean that."

A. J.'s smart-aleck grin faded as he sensed the undercurrent of Harry's words. He could smell it—something big . . . and terrifying. "So . . . why are you here?" he asked quietly.

———

Harry's chosen few filed into Mission Control, joking and laughing despite the poker-faced military escorts who surrounded them. Inside the door they were greeted by Harry Stamper, who introduced them all to Truman.

"You'd better tell me what's going on," Chick said, " 'cause I just got pulled off my first winning streak in six years. So am I pissed? Oh, yeah."

"What's up, Harry?" Bear asked. "NASA found oil on Uranus?"

The guys all laughed—except Harry. Silently he and Truman led them all into the conference room. Their scruffy appearance seemed incongruous reflected in the large, highly polished conference table.

As the lights slowly went down, somebody—Harry wasn't sure who—hissed out some crack about "where's the damned popcorn," but one by one, the guys fell silent as they began to watch the same incredible story that Harry had already been introduced to. In fact, Harry had never seen the guys so quiet. *Maybe somebody ought to check to make sure they're breathing.* He glanced around at the faces he knew so well, tough faces, not afraid of hard work, not quick to be scared by anything. And in the light reflected from the screen he saw the entire kaleidoscope of emotions that he himself had so recently experienced: shock, fascination, disbelief . . . terror.

At last the short presentation ended, and the lights slowly came back up.

Dead silence.

Dan Truman waited a moment for comment, some kind of reaction, but none was forthcoming. "So there it is," he said as calmly as if he were giving a talk at some high school career day. "Any questions?"

"Yeah," Max breathed. "You sure you got the right guys?"

Harry shot Truman a look. "I need to talk to 'em. Alone."

Truman thought a half second, then simply nodded and ushered the NASA people out the door.

When the door clicked shut, Harry turned back to his men, waiting for somebody to say something— anything. But still they sat, silent, stunned, each looking as if he'd been hit in the face with a two-by-four.

And then he saw a crack in the ice. A glimpse of a smile curled one corner of Oscar's mouth.

And then Noonan's crisp, swaggering Aussie accent rang out across the room: "Surprise, right, mate? This is a joke—it's somebody's birthday." He shot a nervous, pleading look around the conference table. "Please—was anybody born today?" One or two guys shook their heads, and Noonan's tentative smile vanished like spit on a hot rig.

Time to give it to 'em straight, Harry decided. "Yeah, this is the craziest shit I ever heard of, too," he said. "And if we choose not to go . . . we're just sitting around waiting for some goddamned rock to kill everything we know. So I'm going. But not one of you needs to prove how tough you are. I've seen you do stuff that would make Neil Armstrong piss his spacesuit. So if you don't think you can make it all the way, I need to know who's in, who's out—right now."

Again, total silence. This was new for this crew.

But then Chick kicked back in his chair and shrugged. "Twenty years, I haven't turned you down once. Not about to start now. I'm there."

Harry smiled.

"Space?" Noonan said, his accent making it sound like *spice.* "I don't know, man. . . ."

"This whole thing's just a little too freaky, isn't it?" Bear whispered.

"No," Oscar responded. "This is just goddamn historic! This is space! *Outer* space! Deep blue hero stuff! Hell, yeah, I'm in!"

Rockhound rubbed his face, leaned forward on the polished conference table, and cleared his throat. "I don't mean to be the materialistic bastard of the group," he said, "but do you think we can get some hazard pay outta this?"

Out in the hallway, Truman, Kimsey, and a handful of other NASA techs stood around waiting, the ticking of the clock like a time bomb inside their heads, each second a giant leap forward toward the end of the future.

Truman and Kimsey were skimming through the files of the wild bunch Harry Stamper had chosen to save all mankind. Confidence was in short supply to say the least.

"This guy Chick was Air Force Commando for six years. . . ." Truman pointed out, holding out the file.

General Kimsey shook his head in disgust. "If you're trying to make me feel better about this scenario, give it up," he growled. "Robbery, assault, arrest, *resisting* arrest. We've got a collection agent for the mob, lewd and salacious conduct in a telephone booth, two of these guys have done serious time—"

"General," Truman interrupted as politely as he could, "they're the best at what they do."

"So am I," the general said. "And I'm *not* an optimist. We spend two hundred and fifty billion dollars a year on defense. We've got ten trillion in technology, thirty years modern training, and here we are. The future of the planet depends on a bunch of retards I wouldn't trust with a potato gun."

"NASA's been warning for twenty years that a cosmic event like this was conceivable," Truman shot back. "They world was too busy investing in Microsoft to listen."

Suddenly the door to the conference room swung

open, and Harry Stamper, followed by his mangy crew, strode into the hallway. All eyes were on them, but their tough faces were unreadable.

Were they in?

Or out?

Truman swallowed the unprofessional choke of fear in his throat and asked, "What's the verdict?"

Harry shrugged. "They'll do it."

Truman sighed in relief and felt the knot in his gut unknot a bit.

"But they have a few requests."

Truman's stomach began to churn again. "Such as?"

Harry attempted to suppress a grin as he held up a written list and very dramatically unfolded it. And unfolded it again. And continued unfolding it until General Kimsey nearly erupted in rage.

Truman silenced the general with a look.

"There's a lot here...." Harry began. "They mostly involve things like ..." He skimmed the list. "Oscar here's got some outstanding parking tickets. Wants 'em wiped off his record."

"Fifty-six tickets," Oscar clarified, "in seven states."

Truman traded looks with Kimsey, then shrugged. "Uh, yeah ... all right."

"Noonan's got two woman friends he'd like to see made American citizens," Harry went on, "no questions asked. Chick wants a week Emperor Package at Caesar's Palace." Harry shrugged again. "That kind of stuff." He presented the list to Truman, waiting for a reaction. Truman skimmed the list, a little taken aback. But his face told Harry what he wanted to hear. The man knew he was in no position to argue—not if he wanted someplace to sit his butt down a month from now.

"These, uh...huh. I guess we can deal with these," Truman said at last.

But then Rockhound cleared his throat, catching Harry's attention. The crew went into a huddle, whispering. Harry nodded his pleased approval, then walked back toward Truman and the general. "And they don't want to pay taxes again."

The general's eyes bugged out.

"Ever," Harry added.

General Kimsey pivoted and stalked off before he did something that he'd regret—something that might interfere with Harry Stamper heading the most important space mission in the history of the Earth.

CHAPTER FIVE

Almost before the ink had dried on their demands list, Harry and his guys were dragged off to NASA's medical examination clinic.

"Over the next several days," Truman told them, "you men will be subjected to a battery of physical, mental, and training exercises for twenty hours a day. Preparing you to survive space travel."

It turned out to be everything Truman promised and more. Every morning they ran. And then they ran tests. And worked out, and ran, and then they ran some more.

"Jesus," Chick said. "You okay, Freddy?"

"Yeah, I'm fine," Noonan replied. "Except for my entire ass."

The head nurse stepped out the door, her rubber-gloved hands holding an enema probe and a jar of Vaseline. "Mr. Chapple, you're next!"

"Look, lady, I just came here to drill," Chick protested.

"Yeah, well, so did she," said Noonan.

———————

A couple of doors down, Harry and A. J. sat on examining tables as two NASA doctors checked their blood pressure and passed the time in geekspeak.

"So I say, 'The adoption of a multidisciplinary approach integrating biological, social, and physical-mathematical research is the primary matrix.' And do you know what Carver says?"

"What?"

"He says, 'Only in a manner consonant with national plans!' "

Then they both cracked up.

A. J. shot Harry a disgusted look. "You know, Harry, I think you're right," he said sarcastically. "I think Grace would be much better off with a doctor or a scientist."

Harry gave him a cold stare.

———————

The whole team threw the guys in psychological testing for a loop.

"Since my wife and I split," Chick was saying, "I get off the job, find a hotel, cash my check, gamble till it hurts, then back to work. Some people might think that's sad. But I say...yeah, I guess it is sad...."

Depressive.

"I don't try to get into fights," Noonan was explaining. "Fights come to me. I'm like flypaper, but for fights. I'm fightpaper. Does that make any sense?"

Psychotic.

"My favorite dish is haggis," Max said. "It's all the parts of the sheep you normally throw away—heart, lungs, liver. You shove it into the sheep's stomach with oats and onions, then you boil it. Little sour cream, Tabasco, that's the best."

Delusional.

"Things I don't like about people?" Oscar sat back and thought a moment. "I don't like people who only read war books. I don't like people who excessively use the word *evidently*. And I don't like people who think Jethro Tull is actually a guy in the band...."

Obsessive.

"Why did my marriage fail?" Harry asked, pissed. "What kind of question is that? Is my ex-wife coming with us? You know, screw you—why did *your* marriage fail?"

Aggressive.

"You want to compare brain pans?" Rockhound asked. "I won the Westinghouse prize when I was twelve. Big deal. Published at nineteen. So what? I got a double doctorate from M.I.T. at twenty-two. Chemistry and geology. I taught at Princeton for two and a half years. So why do I do this, right? This incredibly pedestrian application of my academic credentials, what happened to me, right? Why do I do this? Because the money's good. The scenery changes. And they let me use explosives. Okay?"

Place under observation.

———

Harry recognized this as the old familiar BOG-SATT (bunch of guys sitting around a table talking). Truman, General Kimsey, Quincy, a bunch of other NASA staff guys that Harry didn't know by name, and all the NASA doctors that he and his guys had gotten to know over the past few days.

A Dr. Banks was looking over the test results with a grim expression on his face. "Failed... failed ... impressively failed.... One toxicology analysis revealed Ketamine." At Truman's questioning look, the doctor explained, "That's a very powerful sedative."

Harry shrugged. "Doctor, sedatives are used all the time."

"Yeah, well, this one's used on horses." The doctor paused long enough to let that sink in, then proceeded. "We normally have eighteen months to psychologically prepare pre-screened, viable subjects for space travel. We've seen evidence of a wide variety of inappropriate antisocial behaviors and territorial aggression."

Truman waved all that away and leaned forward

across the table. "Can they physically survive the trip?" he asked bluntly. "That's all we need to know."

"Personally," Dr. Banks replied dryly, "I don't know how they survived the tests." He stared down at the prim black FAILED stamped across the guys' files, sighed, then stamped a much larger red APPROVED on top.

And suddenly it was all real, all true. It was actually going to happen. Harry and his guys were going to make like astronauts and blast off into space. *Holy shit.*

CHAPTER SIX

Colonel Roger Sharp watched Harry and his scruffy band of roughnecks saunter toward him along the scrubbed NASA hallway and felt his jaw flex involuntarily. He was a hardened military and aeronautic veteran, a man used to leading the best of the best.

And this is what they handed him for implementing the most important mission of his entire career.

"We're clean out of options here, Colonel Sharp," Truman said out of the side of his mouth.

"Sir," Sharp responded, gesturing at the strange crew, "you're telling me that my wife and little girl's lives are in their hands?"

"Colonel Sharp," Truman said patiently, "unless you know how to drill, your orders are to train them, land them on that rock, and let 'em do their thing. And by the way ... I've got a family myself."

He knew exactly how Sharp felt.

Inside one of the huge hangars at Edwards Air Force Base, Harry and his guys watched as Colonel Sharp walked past a table overflowing with books and files and studies, shoving them to the floor. "Safety training—irrelevant. Emergency training—no point. Repair, rescue—forget it. If we fail...if we screw up...everyone dies." He looked up at his "class" with a hardened look in his eyes. "Good morning."

Harry and his men nodded.

"United States astronauts train for years. You have twelve days. In addition to flying one of the X-71 teams to that rock, my job's to train you how to deal with the mental and physical rigors of working in space so you don't freak out on the asteroid. Not only do we find ourselves up the creek without a paddle, gentlemen, but the creek's full of piranhas, and we've got stomach cancer. Any intelligent questions before we get started?"

"Yeah," Bear piped up. It was the first one on all their minds. "How do you take a dump in space?"

Chick raised his hand. "What's an X-71?"

"I'm being serious!" Bear said.

Truman groaned and ran a hand through his hair. It was worse than he thought.

———

As much as he hated to, it was time to show these cowboys their horse.

They led them, along with Grace, to NASA's

massive VAB (vehicle assembly building). As the huge doors slid open on the football-field-sized hangar, Harry's jaw fell open.

It was an image straight out of *Stars Wars*, only this was real.

The X-71 space shuttle.

A huge monster of a ship, like something out of the future, gleaming white and surrounded by dozens of technicians who crawled on ladders, platforms, and scaffolding, busting ass to get the thing ready to fly.

"You're the first civilians to ever see her," Truman announced. "Top secret joint venture with the Air Force . . . she and her sister ship at Vanderberg will leave tomorrow for launch prep in Florida. But I thought you should have a look."

Harry hoped he didn't look as dumbstruck as the other guys as they followed Truman over to a crowd of uniforms: Sharp and some other pilots.

"Air Force Colonel Davis and NASA Pilot Tucker will command the shuttle *Independence*. Air Force Colonel Sharp and NASA Pilot Watts will take the shuttle *Freedom*. Munitions Specialists Gruber and Halsey will supervise the nuclear ordnance."

"Once you land on the asteroid, you'll be using our very special drill unit," Quincy said.

"Yeah, where'd you get that beautiful drill design?" Harry asked.

"We call it the Monster Armadillo," Quincy replied.

Harry, Grace, and the guys watched a huge plastic sheet being raised, revealing the two Armadillos. Lower, larger, much, much cooler than the old lunar golf carts from the Apollo days.

"Fourth generation surface rover," Truman explained. "Pressurized titanium alloy air-locked cab. Able to climb an eighty-degree incline. Six-cell solar engine. It'll turn eight hundred turbo horses in near-zero gravity."

"Whoa...." Harry said. "No kidding. Can we take a look?"

Truman nodded his approval.

Minutes later metal pieces came flying out of the guts of the Armadillos as Harry's guys crawled all over, under, inside, and out of the metal creature.

"Grace," Harry hollered to his daughter, who stood nearby with a clipboard, "we need half a dozen full-package, 980 Mack truck transmissions." As Grace nodded and scribbled down every word, Harry shouted, "A. J.! I want you to check into some high-load, waste-gate diaphragms and a couple nine-tooth T5 drive gears."

"Make sure we get stall ratings fifteen hundred under peak and some Hurst five-speed short throw shifters," Chick shouted.

Harry listened to somebody down inside the Armadillo, then shouted to Grace, "Eight diesel, dual-pump point tachs." He listened again, then added,

"Two rolls of Kevlar header wrap. Box of nine-inch graphite U-joints." He paused once more, then added, "Eight buckets of fried chicken. Original Recipe."

Quincy and his men stood watching—speechless, frozen to the spot, and turning pale.

———————

A T-38 fighter jet screamed skyward, giving its occupants a stimulating representation of actual spaceflight.

Seated in the fetal position near the rear of the aircraft was Bear, crammed next to Rockhound, whose eyes were bugging out.

A. J. supplemented his safety restraints and harnesses with an extra firm grip on his seat cushion while Harry made a supreme effort to hold down his Original Recipe.

Through it all they heard the cheerful and satanic voice of their pilot and instructor, a tough Vietnam vet named Chuck Jr. "I will suck your eyes to the back of your heads, flip you, spin you, splat your bodies till your bones hurt—and when you squeal, I'll just do it faster and harder!"

Oscar liked this very much.

"Your spaceflight's gonna be a brutal assault on your senses!" Chuck Jr. hollered at them. "I'm gonna give you a taste of that!"

When the ride was over, Harry was the first to stumble out of the plane, fall to his knees, and kiss the ground. Chuck Jr. wasn't surprised: It was not at all unusual for a T-38 passenger to develop homesickness.

———— ————

Meanwhile, in the Mission Control asteroid-monitoring hub, Truman, Rockhound, Oscar, and Grace were busy studying printouts of the asteroid's surface.

"Based on the thermographic imaging," Rockhound said, "Segment 201, Lateral Grid Six, site 12J14—that's one prime landing site. Site 12G17's another."

Just then Clark hurried over to Truman and drew him aside, speaking quietly. "There's a problem. The shuttle engines might not fire. We might not even be able to get them off the ground."

Truman was getting awfully good at wearing a mask of composure over frustration and rage. "Well, look," he said intensely, "when you get the problem fixed—tomorrow? Then it won't be a problem anymore."

———— ————

The next day, Sharp stood on the stairway of a NASA Boeing 707 and looked over the men boarding the plane with barely contained contempt.

Now at least they were dressed properly—it was a start. They'd been divided into two teams for the mission, designated by either red or blue markings on their flight suits. Harry, Rockhound, Chick, and Max were the blue team, A. J., Bear, Oscar, and Noonan were red.

"Hope you Mission Specialists had a nice relaxing lunch," Sharp said with a satisfied look. "Welcome to the Vomit Comet. Eight days from today you'll feel it for real . . . so today we're gonna fly this bird to forty thousand feet and drop to ten thousand in thirty seconds for weightless training."

Eight miles up the plane stopped rising and dropped like a stone. Harry and his roughnecks rose in the air, weightless. Much more fun than the T-38, until—*ANHHHH!* A buzzer sounded and the crew dropped to the deck like anvils.

After the flight the crew rushed for the men's room, validating the vehicle's name. Harry threw up in the sink as Rockhound looked on: "I was talking to this hotty in the metabolic secretions department. I'm working her, all right? So don't repeat this, this is secret." He coughed a little, but managed not to throw up, and went on. "Basically, the closer this rock gets, the more they're learning and the less they're liking—I'm talking about gas volcanoes and ice storms and seismic crap and rock slides and shit I can't even bring myself to say—" The sounds of fresh heaving distracted him a moment, then he turned back to Harry. "Not only are we landing on a psycho-bitch of an asteroid—that's not the secret. The secret is those shuttles that they've never flown. They've done four hundred flight simulations, right?

Take a freakin' guess how many of those sim-launches worked."

Harry splashed water from the spigot into his mouth, gargled, and spit, then leaned over the side of the bowl. "Just tell me it's more than once."

"Did she tell you that? Once. Bingo. You win the shit-prize: You get to come with me."

———————

The revamped Armadillo sat in a dry lake bed outside the city of Houston. Harry and his crew had re-created it in their own image, and now he and A. J. were taking it for a test spin, with Quincy on hand to give them pointers. If the NASA official was aware of the tension between the two men, he didn't let on.

"Now I'll ask you to lock the brakes," Quincy instructed.

Harry hit the five switches to activate the brake lock.

"Good," Quincy said. "Now I'll ask you to re-verse thrusters—safety's on. . . ."

A. J. began the thrust procedure. "Can I ask you something?" The words were aimed at Harry, not at the instructor.

Harry grimaced. "If the words *Grace, daughter, love, dating,* or *Harry, please* are about to come out of your mouth, I don't want to hear it." He yanked the throttle.

Quincy's eyes nearly popped out. "Wait— don't—"

Suddenly the Armadillo rumbled to life. Its giant grounding pincers swung wide, slamming onto the hard, parched ground. Harry and A. J. were thrown against the cockpit wall.

Quincy hit his head hard. "Well, that's why we wear seat belts," he lectured.

———————

Late that evening in NASA's old Mission Control, Oscar sat at the out-of-service control console imagining what it must have been like during the early days. He slipped an ancient-looking headset on and pretended to work the controls. Unknown to him, Harry had slipped into the room, and he watched quietly for a moment as Oscar spoke: "Apollo, this is Houston. Engage landing gear booster rockets, over." Like a boy at play, he cupped his hands and made a sound like static. "Apollo, we do not copy, repeat, do not copy, over."

"Hey—" Harry interrupted.

Oscar jumped a foot, totally embarrassed as he turned to find Harry watching him. "I was just here . . . feeling the history, you know? Taking it in. This is epic, Harry. Truly epic—"

"You seen Grace?" was all Harry could say.

Oscar nodded his head, glad to be talking about something else. "Yeah, she was with A. J. in that hangar, you know those huge rock——" He broke off suddenly as he saw a color best described as rage red flood Harry's cheeks. "Oh, wait! Grace? No, no, that wasn't her. That was, uh ..."

But Harry shot from the room before Oscar could finish making up his lame cover-up.

Oscar winced. "Sorry, A. J.," he muttered as he jumped to his feet. The way Harry was looking, Oscar had a feeling the couple might need some backup.

———————

The blood was pounding a war chant in Harry's brain as he charged toward the Saturn 5 hangar, and it escalated to World War III when he found his daughter and A. J. huddled before some candles, locked in a sweaty embrace. Damn, Grace was even wearing a dress. He opened his mouth——then clamped it shut as Oscar came up behind him. Then Chick. Then Rockhound.

Harry shook his head and turned away, and Oscar, Chick, and Rockhound followed him out. The lovestruck couple didn't even notice.

Outside, Harry strode through the orbiter processing facility under the belly of a mothballed space shuttle, heading back to the barracks. His men tried to keep up. "What am I, the Pied Piper?" he shot back over his shoulder.

"We were just wondering," Chick began, "after we save the world, will Grace be grounded?"

"Just get out of my face," Harry growled.

"Grace is old enough to vote," Chick argued. "And drink and get married and get divorced and . . . you know . . . whenever, whatever she wants . . . if she wants."

"Thank you, Dr. Spock."

"The man's right, Harry." Bear spoke up.

"Fine!" Harry said. "He's right. The next two weeks they can do whatever they want, I don't care. But when we get back, when this is all done, I'm gonna deal with it. My way."

"Not like I'm rooting for A. J., here, Harry, but come on," Rockhound argued. "Grace isn't a little girl anymore. Don't mind me saying it, but while we were running around the globe, hunting mud, little Gracie went and turned into a fullgrown hotty—"

"I know who and what my daughter is, okay? I'm not as dumb as I look."

"The point is," Oscar said, "You've gotta let her live her life—"

"You're five minutes older than she is, Oscar," Harry shot back. "Why does any of this concern you?"

"Well, Harry," Bear put in, "all due respect and shit, but . . . we kinda feel like we helped in raisin' her, too—"

"Yeah? Well, you did a hell of a job, 'cause right now she's exchanging uvulas with a reckless rough-neck whose attitude sucks!" He stopped and jammed his hands on his hips, looking around at Grace's other "parents." "Look at you guys. Look at me. Living in goddamn shacks floating in the middle of nowhere, never on land for more than an eight-week stretch, covered in filth most of the time. Our lives are dangerous. And lonely." And when he looked at them, the anger in his eyes melted into something different, something softer. "Grace," he said simply, "is better than us. She is. Understand?"

"In six days we're going into space," Chick said. "No kidding?"

"This isn't just another job in the South China Sea," Chick persisted, ignoring Harry's sarcasm. "Now, Rockhound's right. We've got about zero odds of surviving this. You know that. So here's a piece of unasked-for advice: Figure it all out with your 'little girl.' You know? Just in case."

Harry glared at them, all nodding in agreement. But he was pissed. "Thank you! No, really. Look at you guys. You've got seven divorces, a pack of kids, most of whom don't even know your names, and a dozen years in county lock-up between you. And *you're* giving *me* advice? I've gotta take advice on how to relate to my daughter from a bunch of drunken mud-hunters who consider meaningful emotional contact to be tucking dollar bills into G-strings?"

He looked up and appealed to the gods and then said in closing, "Thanks for the advice, guys. Thanks a pant's load. Now, if you'll excuse me, I have to go back to my room, open a vein, and mull over these pearls of Oprah-worthy wisdom you've given me...."

Oscar, Chick, and Rockhound looked sheepishly at one another. Damn, but Harry sure knew how to make a guy feel like shit....

CHAPTER SEVEN

The next morning, NASA's Jennifer Watts introduced Harry and his crew to the Johnson Vacuum Chamber by first showing classic black-and-white footage of Neil Armstrong working on the surface of the moon. The guys looked competent in their flight suits, but Watts had to try to ignore the fact that Rockhound kept whispering to Bear during the movie.

"This'll be very much like the gravitational conditions on the asteroid. If you set an object down, it'll stay put. But up there, what goes up ... keeps going. These new-generation suits have directional accelerant thrusters—*Bear!*" she suddenly shouted, whipping her head around to give him the evil eye. "Do we have a problem? I'm trying to explain how these DAT's keep your ass on the ground! Which means if I were to kick you in the balls and you weren't wearing it, you'd do what?"

"Float away?" Bear guessed nervously.

Rockhound raised his hand, and Watts called on him.

"When do we start training for *that*?" he asked.

Watts's answer was to jab a button on the controls, and slowly the massive, forty-ton door to the chamber began to close. "Get your helmets on," Watts warned them, "'cause all the oxygen's gonna be sucked out of this vacuum in eighteen seconds. Just like in space."

The guys quit fooling around and fumbled for their helmets as the door slammed shut.

"Harry," Rockhound said through his helmet. "What are you thinking?"

Harry eyed the six-story-tall wind tunnel fans at the end of the chamber. "I don't care how bad it gets down here...up there, they don't have an off switch."

And at that moment the fans switched on and blew them like autumn leaves across the room.

———

"I don't need any more bad news," Truman told the geo technician who'd come over with some reports.

The woman shrugged. "She's starting to show her personality," she said of the asteroid. "The atmosphere's brutal—severe windstorms peaking at a hundred and thirty miles an hour, sir."

"So..." Truman said grimly. "Give me some good news. Please."

"My son's three today," the technician said with a bittersweet smile.

———————   ———————

Out of the blackness of space the asteroid sped toward Earth, surrounded by many satellite-like rocks.

———————   ———————

On the NASA clock, the time to global impact read: 174:12:18:028.

CHAPTER EIGHT

Jules Verne, where are you when we need you? Truman thought cynically as he met the next day with the far-from-meshed team of roughnecks and NASA technicians. Deep down in his gut he feared the only way any of them would ever be ready for a successful mission was if he could stuff the whole crew into some kind of time machine and hurl them back five or ten years—*at least*—to a time when an increase in NASA funding might have given them time and a little more than a snowball's chance in hell of developing—and properly testing—an intelligent defense against an asteroid crashing into the Earth.

But it was impossible to go back, too late to regret history. *Two roads diverged in a yellow wood, and sorry I—*

Too late to be sorry. All he had was right now and the future. What little there might be left of it. That and the small army of people who stood before him.

It would have to do.

Truman shook himself and referred to the informal models they'd constructed, styro balls tethered on clear fishing line. "The flight plan goes like this: Both shuttles take off Tuesday at 8:14 A.M. Twenty-seven minutes later shuttles will dock with the Russian space station. You'll refill on liquid O-2. That's your fuel. You'll release and take a sixty-hour trip toward the moon. We've only got one shot of landing on the rock, and that's when it passes by the moon. Then you'll use lunar gravity to double your speed—we're gonna slingshot you around the moon—you'll hit upwards of eleven Gs—"

"Oh, I remember this one," Harry piped up. "The coyote sat his ass in a slingshot and strapped an Acme rocket to his back. But it didn't turn out so good." He chuckled, stuffing his hands in his pockets as he looked around at the stony faces of the NASA people. *What—are we all too scared shitless to even laugh anymore?* He shrugged and grinned at Truman. "That's sorta what we're doing here, right?"

"We've got better rockets than Acme, Stamper," Truman said, dead serious. "So after the Roadrunner move, you'll be traveling at twenty-two thousand five hundred miles an hour, you'll come around behind the asteroid, where we are hoping the tail debris will be cleared by the moon's gravity. You'll land right here," he said, pointing with a pencil at the tiny ball that was supposed to be the asteroid. "That's it."

Oscar raised his hand and asked, "Let's say for

a second we actually *do* land on the thing . . . what's it gonna be like?"

Truman gave it to him straight. "Two hundred degrees in sunlight, minus two hundred in shade. Canyons of razor-sharp rock. Unstable ground, unclear gravitational conditions, unpredictable eruptions——"

"Oh," Oscar interrupted, nodding, "so, the scariest environment imaginable. Thanks." He shrugged. "All you had to say was 'scariest environment imaginable.'"

Truman moved toward a monitor and hit the play button on his remote computer control. He explained the images as computer graphics conveyed the simple procedure. "You drill, you drop the nuke, you leave. Now, here's the key: You'll remote-detonate the bomb before the asteroid passes this plane: Zero Barrier. You do that, and the remaining pieces of rock will be deflected enough to slide right by us."

The imaginary computer graphics scenario showed two giant asteroid halves just missing the Earth.

"If the asteroid passes Zero Barrier and the bomb hasn't exploded . . ."

The room fell silent as all eyes watched the monitor in dread. The computer graphic bomb discharged past Zero Barrier, and both pieces of the asteroid crashed into the Earth.

"Game's over," Truman summarized.

No one spoke. Few even breathed.

Truman pointed toward two bar graphs that next appeared. " 'Time to Zero Barrier' and 'Depth.' If this gauge runs out first, you don't have a hole. I'd say you could just go home," he shrugged, "but you won't have that, either."

———————

When the briefing broke up, and the room's occupants scattered to their various tasks, a grim, thoughtful Truman remained behind with Quincy, Sharp, and Davis.

"Just getting those two shuttles off the ground's gonna be a minor miracle," he said. "We've never done it. That's one hurdle. Then double-docking with the space station, transferring eight tons of O-2, flammable as all hell . . . that's one big-ass hurdle. And whipping two birds behind the moon— hitting G-forces that could kill a man . . . that's a goddamned hurdle. And then we've got the hard part. Landing both vehicles on a rock blazing through the universe for God knows how long." He looked at the others, wondering if they even got it. "Do you realize what we're setting out to do here?"

Nobody said a word. Yeah, they got it, all right.

———————

Dusk enveloped the dry lake bed where the two Armadillos crouched like aliens. If the whole scenario weren't so horrifying, Harry thought, this might al-most be fun.

"I asked for twice the equipment, but this is all that'll fit," Harry explained to his crew. "Each team's got a thousand feet of pipe, two trannies, and five drill bits. Once we land we've got eight hours. That's a quick forty-five minutes of setup, six and a half hours of ass-breaking drill time, then forty-five minutes to drop the nuke and take off. In order to tap this fault line to split this rock in half, we're gonna need nothing less than an hour. That's tough. Let's go to simulation."

———————

Soon the red team was suited up and immersed in the neutral buoyancy tank, which was designed to somewhat simulate the conditions they'd be working under on the asteroid. Harry monitored them with a stopwatch as they moved to adjust the mock-up drill arm.

"All right, we're going for a bit change!" Harry shouted. "Bear, clamp it down! Okay, hurry, hurry, hurry! You guys gotta do this faster up there! Load the pipe, Oscar! A. J., let's up the torque!"

A. J. revved the drill, the clock ticked, and a CG screen simulated the drill depth and rpm's as gloved hands pulled cable, clamped pipe, and went back for more.

Sweat poured down Bear's face as he strained to

feed pipe fast enough to keep up with the drill. "A. J.! Slow it down, man!"

Truman watched them with a keen eye on the countdown clock.

"She can handle this," A. J. shot back. "Can you? I'm taking her up!"

"A. J.," Harry shouted, "you're at six hundred feet, your pipe is long, so pull her back to eight thousand rpm's!"

"We don't have time for eight thousand!" A. J. yelled.

"Take her back," Harry ordered, "or you'll snap the pipe or blow the tranny!"

But A. J. was hell-bent on playing it his way. "Come on, guys, keep it up! We're the younger team! I'm going to eleven thousand! Bear, give the turbine more O-2!"

The drive was shaking like crazy, stress loading in the machinery.

"Harry," Bear choked out, "you listening to this?"

"A. J., you're gonna blow the tranny!" Harry shouted. "Back off *now!*"

"More O-2, Bear!" A. J. shouted as if he hadn't even heard Harry's orders. "You're on my team now! This is how it's gonna be!"

Suddenly A. J.'s meters jumped and the computer alarm sounded—he'd blown the tranny.

Harry punched his fist into his other hand. "*All right, get him out! Pull him up!*"

As soon as A. J. was pulled free from the water, Harry stormed over, grabbed him, and slammed him against the wall. Chick ran over to break it up, but Harry just shoved him out of the way. "*Your team?*" Harry screamed, inches from A. J.'s startled face. "*Your team* just blew the transmission!"

"That NASA wimp computer's *wrong*," A. J. sputtered, struggling to free himself from Harry's grip. "Your machine—the real thing—*she can take it!*"

"Well, that damn rock is no place to find out!" Harry shot back. "We've got very limited resources up there! There's no room for hot-dogging, showing off, going with instinct, or trying to be a hero, you got that?" He shook A. J. against the wall. "Tell me you got it. *Say the words!*"

"I got it, I got it!" A. J. answered angrily. "Christ!"

Harry jabbed a finger at him, almost up his nose. "I want you to go back in there and do it my way, no fight, no ego, no questions asked!"

Minutes later, A. J. was back in the water, working the drill, with Harry manning the stopwatch again, giving the orders. And the wisdom of strategy was soon evident to all who were watching. The computer graphics monitor showed the drilling at 8,000 rpm's hitting 800 feet.

It worked.

Harry didn't gloat, but nodded with the satisfaction of a professional whose calculations based on years of learning, experience, and gut instincts had successfully worked a problem against the odds.

But he tensed up as he felt Truman and Sharp move in on him like bookends.

"If you want to replace a member of the crew," Sharp said, "now *is* the time."

Harry ignored him. In spite of what had happened—in spite of the fact he'd like to boot A. J.—nobody told him who and who not to use on a job—any job. "I'm making a change in the schedule," he said curtly. "My guys, they get tomorrow night off."

Truman blanched. "What do you mean, *off?*"

"I mean *out of here,*" Harry explained, as if Truman were deaf or an idiot or both. "One night. Ten hours. Then we go to Kennedy."

"Harry, I can't do that," Truman protested incredulously. "There's too much at stake. What if they get hurt? What if they talk?"

Harry turned on him, his eyes full of fire and ice. "What if they're too burned out to do the right thing? What if they're so tense they snap? What if they forget what they're fighting for?" When he saw Truman take a step backward, he reined himself in some, but didn't change his mind. "You want their best, you've gotta let 'em blow. I'm not asking. I'm telling."

One day later to the hour, the NASA security gates swung open, and Harry and his crew were set loose on the town in a limo.

CHAPTER NINE

"You sure you don't want to check it?" The loan shark picked up the last pile of money from an electric cash counter and laid the thick stack on the table. He looked at the guy in front of him skeptically.

"Nah, looks like a hundred grand to me," Rockhound said, stuffing the cash into a wrinkled paper bag.

The loan shark grabbed his wrist and stared him square in the eye. "Sixty percent interest. No excuses, no extensions—you understand that? Or some of your fingers are gonna be mine."

"Yadda, yadda, yadda," Rockhound yapped. "You know where to find me. Yeah, I got it."

Suddenly the loan shark's eyes bulged open wide. "Hey, you're not . . . sick, are you? Dying and shit?"

Rockhound shrugged as he headed for the door. "Let's just say, no more than you are."

Where does a meteorite park in Manhattan?
Anywhere it wants to. *The car-sized boulders that did this are nothing compared to the asteroid that's on the way!*

NASA's Dan Truman (Billy Bob Thornton) lays it on the line for oil driller Harry Stamper (Bruce Willis) and his crew—destroy the asteroid before the asteroid destroys us. "Any questions?" Max (Ken Campbell) asks what's on everyone's mind: "You sure you got the right guys?"

*Dressed to drill: A. J. (Ben Affleck), Oscar (Owen Wilson),
and Bear (Michael Duncan) in NASA uniforms.*

Fiery Grace Stamper (Liv Tyler), Harry's daughter, is a chip off the old block.

The *Armadillo* surface rover climbs surfaces up to 80 degrees steep behind 800 turbo horses in near-zero gravity. Perfect for space or around town.

NASA officials look on in horror as Harry's jacks-of-all-trades make a few minor adjustments to the equipment.

Fasten seat belts, please—it's Watts (Jessica Steen) behind the wheel.

A NASA tech's worst nightmare is an angry Stamper. Grace doesn't like finding out that NASA has stolen her dad's drill design.

Here's the plan: Your guys leave Earth in two orbiters, intercept a Texas-sized asteroid on the other side of the moon, then plant and detonate a nuclear warhead. Is it a deal? Harry and Truman shake on it.

America's dream team; Earth's only hope.

With both A. J. and her father at risk, reflective Grace wishes for nothing less than a perfect mission.

Harry never signed up to save the planet, but he's sure stuck with the job now!

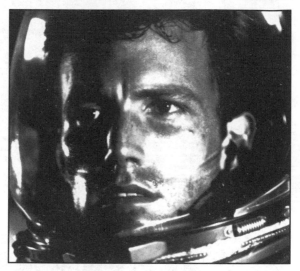

A. J. prepares for a heroic journey.

*All suited up and no place to go—at the last minute,
Harry discovers that the nuke is malfunctioning.*

In a straw vote, A. J. gets elected to stay behind.

Judgment day:
Chick (Will Patton) and Harry must make an executive decision—
with Earth's fate resting in the balance.

As soon as they'd sprung him, Harry Stamper had headed straight for his house, and now he browsed through his small office, which was crammed full of photographs, mementos, trophies, and pieces of old equipment from years in the drilling business. He picked up several pictures of Grace as a little girl and gazed at them. Try as hard as he might, that was how he still saw her: young, cute as a button, and full of youthful innocence. Did any father ever look at his daughter any other way?

Shaking his head, Harry pulled open a desk drawer and reached for the old Bible he kept there.

Then his eye fell on the old black-and-white photo of him as a kid, with his dad covered in oil next to the old Airstream silver bullet camper. Harry grinned and tucked the aging photo into the pages of the Bible, then hurried from the room.

The sun was setting when he pulled up to his dad's cottage and got a quick kiss from the nurse just for showing up. "How is he?" Harry asked, nodding toward the old man who sat in a chair on the far side of the room.

The nurse grinned and shook her head. "Mean as a snake—"

"Tell me something I don't know." Harry strode toward his dad, Hollis Stamper—Grap, they called him, a tough, ancient old bird fighting his oncoming senility with a hearty dose of piss and vinegar.

"How's it hangin'?" Harry asked. "They treating you all right?"

Grap scowled up at his son. "Pills every four hours. Jell-O every five. What is Jell-O, Harry? You know what it is? I'll tell you. It's pudding for sissies. Goddamned pudding for sissies...."

"Hey, it keeps you regular."

"Hell it does!" Grap retorted. "I haven't had a solid crap since Iran had a Shah—"

"Maybe there's a connection."

"They underestimate me, Harry," Grap said, lowering his voice conspiratorially. "They don't know like we know. I'm ready to work, damn it. You got a job comin' up?"

"Yeah, we got one—"

"I've got my boots and gloves," the old man said, moving in his chair as if to get up. "I'm all packed up and ready for a mud-hunt. Tell 'em what kinda people we are. I'm Hollis Vernon Stamper, and I didn't get where I am by doing things part way."

"I'll talk to 'em, Pop," Harry reassured him, settling his dad's frail frame back into his chair.

Suddenly the old man's face softened, and he gazed up into Harry's face. "How's my granddaughter?"

Harry grinned. "Grace!" he hollered, then told his dad, "Dancin' on my heart—"

"Just like her momma." Grap nodded.

"Only without the stiletto heels."

"Yeah, well, the good Lord gave us children so's we'd have roses in December...." Grap pronounced.

Harry's eyebrow shot up. That was rather profound for Grap, and he stared at the man for a good long time.

Grap made a face. "What?"

"I love you, Grap."

The old man seemed surprised, but just as his eyes grew misty, he scowled and hollered, "What kind of shit is that? Prove it, then. Get me some goddamned pudding!" Then his eyes lit up like Christmas, and Harry knew without turning that Grace had entered the room.

With the warm colors of sunset streaming through the screen door across her face, she still looked as pretty as the first time he'd met her, Chick thought as he stood outside on the rough wooden porch of a tiny house in Houston. But now she looked at him with anything but open invitation. "Sorry." Chick felt the need to apologize. "I was just . . ."

She came out of the house then, nervous as she watched his every move. "What? You need money, right?"

"No! Thanks," he said quickly. "Really, I'm flush." Then his eyes strayed past her, through the screen door again, to the six-year-old boy watching him with wide eyes. "He got big," Chick said softly.

"Court says you can't come around like this," she said.

"I know."

"Ma?" The hinges screeched softly as the boy eased open the screen door.

"Get back in the house!" his mother ordered.

"Look, I'm sorry. About everything," Chick said, backing away. Then he blurted out, "I got something coming up . . . you know, you might just be proud of me."

Then he turned and hurried off, with as much longing in his heart as filled the young boy's eyes.

———————

Max Lennert sat at his momma's table doing what he did best—eating like there was no tomorrow. *'Cause there might not be,* Max thought.

He watched his mother working over the stove, which had what seemed like at least a half dozen pots of supper going. He knew he couldn't tell her what he and his pals were about to do, and it pained him greatly, since he'd never kept a secret from his momma in his life. But he couldn't help but talk about it just a little. "Hey, Momma," he said between mouthfuls, "when I was a kid, you ever dream of me growing up and being an astronaut?"

"Nah," his mother said, tossing a handful of something into a sizzling pot. "Never could see you eatin' that freeze-dried crap and drinkin' Tang. Shit."

———————

Oscar spent his night off on his knees—in a church confessional.

───────

At the Alamo Strip Club, Rockhound and Noonan were making up for some of the other guys' quieter pursuits by trying to spend Rockhound's entire hundred grand in a single night out. All the girls had flocked to the VIP section, where Rockhound and Noon were stuffing hundred dollar bills anywhere they felt like it as champagne—the expensive stuff—flowed.

"What brings you to the Alamo?" asked one young lady known as Molly Mounds as she curled against him like a cat.

"Little astronaut training," Rockhound bragged. He shook her hand. "Hound, mission specialist."

"Hey!" shouted a huge customer as he shoved his way through the crowd. "Who the hell do you guys think you are? You're hogging all the action!"

"Hey, pinhead!" Noonan hooted. "Go find your own party."

"Why don't you spread the wealth, pal?" shouted an even bigger guy dressed in leather, chains, and more than his share of muscle.

Rockhound pulled out his wad and peeled off a bill, which he tossed dismissively at his uninvited guest. "Here. Go out and buy yourself a neck."

That did it. As Rockhound ducked behind some strippers, the biker guy threw a punch and Noonan waded into the melee, swinging a bottle as all hell broke loose.

Within forty-five minutes, three squad cars had Rockhound, Noonan, and about ten other guys—bloody, with torn shirts and bruised knuckles—lined up in the alley behind the strip club with their hands up against the brick wall.

"I'm telling you," Rockhound whined, "call NASA. They'll confirm it."

"Yeah," the biker guy chimed in. "We're all astronauts, officer."

The only answer Rockhound got was a little rough stuff from one of the cops.

"Pal," Rockhound complained, "you are *so* messing with national security right now...."

———

NASA people were running like crazy toward some kind of emergency. Harry, just back from his night off, grabbed one by the arm to ask, "Hey, what's going on?"

"Space command spotted more incoming," the guy told him, then ran toward Mission Control.

The room was in an uproar, a mad scramble with lights blinking, phones ringing, people dashing everywhere—with Dan Truman at the epicenter.

"Somebody give me a projected impact!" Truman shouted over the noise.

"East Asia," a tech called out. "Eleven minutes ..."

Clark frantically grabbed a phone. "We've got to warn—"

"Warn who?" Truman snapped. "The whole South Pacific?

———

The busy nighttime harbor in the city of Shanghai was alive with neon lights and floating junks and people in a hurry.

Suddenly a sonic boom cracked the sky, and for a few seconds that seemed like forever, night became day. A terrified young boy reached for his father's hand just as the asteroid shrieked into the harbor, breaking the junks like matchsticks and instantly flash-boiling a million gallons of sea water.

———

Mission Control was as quiet as a tomb. The full impact of the damage was almost impossible for a sane mind to absorb. And yet absorb it they must, for it was a mere preview of what the future held for the entire world if the people in this room failed. Truman felt devastated. But when he saw Harry, he moved toward him with a confident look in his eye. "Do me a favor," he said quietly, "and tell me you've never let anyone down."

Harry rubbed his jaw, trying to decide how truthful to be. "Well..."

"Christ!" Truman exclaimed. "Just lie to me, all right?"

"I've never quit," Harry said at last. "How's that?"

Their eyes met, and for a moment, Truman almost smiled.

"You know, I still remember the first, middle, and last name of every man who qualified for the astronaut program my first year here," Truman said. "Twenty-two years ago. It was different then. Wasn't about the paperwork and politics—just about doing the job right. That was the year we sent up the Viking lander. I joined the engineering program even though all I wanted was to go up. Be one of the guys with the mission patches on his arm, you know?" He shrugged. "Turns out every one of those men dropped out of the Administration years ago. But here I am." He sighed. "I'd be on that shuttle with you, Harry. If I could."

"You don't want to go up any more than I do," Harry told him. "You're afraid . . . because you don't really know what we're up against."

Truman shook his head sadly. "No. I'm afraid . . . because I think I do."

CHAPTER TEN

Chick snapped off a crisp salute to Davis, then climbed onto the plane with Max right behind him. Rockhound and Noonan were dragging. Harry growled as he watched Grace and A. J. head for the plane, entwined.

Truman walked up to Harry. "Local reporter picked up on our radio traffic. Now a French satellite's found the thing. So I have a few thousand calls to make."

"So this is good-bye," Harry said.

Truman stuck his hand out, and the two men shook hands. "Let's not say that," Truman suggested.

"We get through this," Harry said with a slow grin, "you're buying the beer."

Truman nodded. "Hey, I'll even pop for the pretzels. . . ."

As the guys flew toward Kennedy Space Center, the story spread through the media like wildfire.

*. . . rumors circulating all last week about the possibility of
    further strikes . . .*

Senior Pentagon officials refused . . .

*The President returning from Camp David adds fuel to
    the speculation . . .*

*. . . Japanese satellite is now confirming the presence of an
    object . . .*

———————   ———————

Harry and his crew arrived at Kennedy Space
Center at dusk, in time to see a crawler moving a
towering X-71 rocket toward the launch gantry. They
all tumbled out of their ground transport vehicle to
stare up at the massive shuttle.

"You see those things all the time," Oscar said,
shaking his head in awe. "You just never think you're
gonna be in one. . . ."

"Yeah," Noonan breathed, "it's like with super-
models."

———————   ———————

At dawn the next morning, Grace stood at the
Apollo 1 launch site, where Virgil Grissom, Edward
White, and Roger Chaffee were burned alive trapped
inside their capsule before it even took off from the
ground. . . . It looked like a rusted, steel Stonehenge.
She brooded over the wreckage, a relic of a more
innocent age. Harry came up behind her.

"Hey," he called softly.

Grace turned and didn't even try to force a smile. "Thanks for coming."

"Yeah, of course. What's up?"

"I think we have some issues to resolve, don't you?" she asked.

Harry sighed. This wasn't the way he wanted to spend what could be his last moments with his daughter.

"Listen, maybe I overreacted with A. J., but I don't want you to make the same mistakes I did, that's all. Just look at you, Grace. What I see is ... God, help me ... a second chance. Another shot. A big do-over.... You don't have to live this life. You don't have to ramble. You can lay down roots. Raise kids. Have a driveway. Shovel it. Yell at the god-damned paper boy for his bad aim...." His voice trailed off at the sad look that crossed Grace's face.

"No matter what I've said, I've never blamed you for my mother leaving," Grace said softly. "She's just a theory, Harry. You're what I have. I love my life."

And then her arms were around him, hugging him the way she used to when she was a little girl, like she hadn't hugged him for ages. He hugged her back, and almost felt that if he held her tight enough, he could make time stand still and keep the future at bay, like when she used to have nightmares that sent her into his arms. But even daddies couldn't do that, no matter how hard they tried.

"I have two favors to ask you," Grace almost whispered into his shoulder. "They're important."

Harry held her at arm's length and smiled at the

slight quiver that made her normally spunky chin tremble. "Let's hear 'em."

"Don't make this a one-way trip."

Harry swallowed the lump in his throat. "Deal. What's the other one?"

And then the tears welled up and spilled down her cheeks, but even then her gaze didn't waver. "I want you to bring my fiancé back with you."

The news knocked the wind out of Harry for a moment. She wasn't just persisting in a foolish infatuation, wasn't just rebelling to drive her old man crazy. She was in for the long haul this time. And she looked as if she were bracing for another onslaught of Harry's temper.

But instead he surprised not only her but also himself, and just took her into his arms again. Never quick to cry, even as a child, she was doing a pretty good job of soaking his shirt. And then his eyes fell on the plaque that she'd been reading when he first joined her.

1967
DEDICATED TO THE LIVING MEMORY
OF THE CREW OF APOLLO 1

Harry was glad she couldn't see the fear that washed across his face. Would someone be etching a plaque like this for Harry and his crew in the days ahead? Or even worse—would there be no one left this time to remember?

———————

The staff at Mission Control monitored the news as the countdown to takeoff neared.

> *...a secret shuttle project that was to be announced next year...*
> *The President is just about to address the nation from the White House....*

They'd tried their best to keep the disaster under wraps. But television and radio were about to unleash the terror into the living rooms of America.

CHAPTER ELEVEN

Ready or not, here we come.... Harry and his crew were as prepped as they could be, given their deadline, and despite his fear, Harry was pumped to go to work. He and the guys were suited up and waiting for the go-ahead, as NASA technicians and military personnel scurried around them like paparazzi.

Grace had accompanied them every step of the way, but now she could go no farther. She told her makeshift family good-bye, and shot Harry a sweet smile, but couldn't seem to let go of A. J.

"Mr. Frost," a NASA tech called to him. "Are you good to go?"

But A. J. would not have his good-bye to Grace rushed. "Just goin' for a quick spin," he joked. "Should be back in no time."

"It already feels like a lifetime," she whispered.

"Close your eyes," he told her. "Feel this, right now—make this a memory...."

He kissed her—a long, slow kiss.

"Mr. Frost, please," the NASA tech begged.

By now the entire staff of Mission Control was watching as A. J. bid Grace farewell and strolled toward the convoy of vehicles. "I'm marrying you!" he called.

"You bet your ass you are!" she replied with tears in her eyes but a smile on her face.

Harry, watching, had to thank the guy for that as they were all loaded into the transport vehicles. And then they were gone.

———

The President of the United States looked at the television news cameras with what he hoped was his calmest, most reassuring expression. Then he began to read his prepared speech.

"I address you tonight not as the President of the United States, not as the leader of a country, but as a citizen of humanity. We are faced with the greatest of challenges. Some have said we have reached the day the Bible calls Armageddon. The end of all things. And yet, for the first time in the history of the planet, a species possesses the technology to prevent its own extinction."

And as the President spoke, the cameras cut to shots of Harry Stamper and the rest of the flight crew, heroic-looking as they stepped out of the escort vehicles at the gantry base.

Grap Stamper, parked by his nurse in front of

his TV set as always, dropped his Jell-O when he saw Harry's face flash across the screen.

The President went on, "All of you listening and praying with us tonight need to know that everything we can do to prevent this disaster is being called into service...."

In Houston, Chick's little boy called to his mother as Chick's face grinned back at them from the screen.

"That's your daddy," she whispered, staring at the image in shocked disbelief.

"The human thirst for knowledge and excellence; our every step up the ladder of science; every adventurous reach into the heavens; all of our combined modern technologies and imaginations; even the wars we have fought; have given us the tools to wage this terrible battle...."

The gantry elevators closed on the flight teams as launch personnel scurried around the base.

"Through all the chaos that has ever been our history, through all the wrong, and discord, the pain and suffering, through all our times, one thing has nourished our souls and elevated our species above its origins. That is our courage...."

Max's momma watched on her kitchen TV set, her hands clutched to her chest when she saw her baby up there on the screen.

"Tonight, the dreams of an entire planet are focused on the fourteen brave souls traveling into the heavens...."

Alone in his hole-in-the-wall apartment, the loan

shark watched in amazement, and from their own small trailer, Karl and Dottie watched, too.

"Godspeed," the President concluded, "and good luck to you. And may we all, the world over, see these events through with a dignity and perseverance worthy of the challenge."

———————

The sun was just setting, its final rays glinting off the upper gantry T-bar, with *Freedom* to the left and *Independence* to the right. Harry and A. J. were the last to separate into their teams.

"Nice show back there," Harry quipped.

"Thank you," A. J. replied.

"You really this brave?" Harry asked. "Or you just full of it?"

A. J. gave his potential father-in-law a slow, hard look and decided to be straight with the man who up until recently had been like a father to him. "I'm full of it, Harry. Never been so scared in all my life."

Harry grinned. "Good. Me, too. And listen, in case we don't make it, I just want you to know——"

"Harry, man, you don't have to say anything, really."

"——that you've turned out to be a real disappointment. You let me down, kid. One hundred percent."

A. J. was totally, completely stunned. But before he could manage to respond, Harry had walked onto his own shuttle without a look back. Shaking his head, A. J. turned and stepped into his own.

On *Freedom*, strap-in teams in NASA jumpsuits harnessed Harry, Chick, Max, and Rockhound behind Sharp, Watts, and Gruber on the flight deck.

On *Independence*, it was A. J., Noonan, Bear, and Oscar behind Davis, Tucker, and Halsey.

"We're sitting on top of four million pounds of fuel and one nuclear weapon, in a thing that has two hundred and seventy-six thousand moving parts built by the lowest bidder," Rockhound said. "That makes you feel good, doesn't it?"

Nobody cared to answer that.

Oscar rubbed his palms together. "I've got that . . . excited and scared at the same time feeling. You know? Like, ninety-eight percent excited, two percent scared. Or maybe it's two percent excited, and ninety-eight percent scared. I can't tell. That's why it's so cool. That's why it's so intense. 'Cause it's so . . . confusing."

Nobody was listening.

The countdown ticked off the last remaining seconds before the launch sequence, and Truman radioed in over the engineering buzz, "You're our warriors up there, gentlemen. God be with you."

The engines vented and fired and began to pour heavy vapor onto the concrete pad.

Launch Control reported commencing the auto—ground launch sequencer, and Sharp gave them the go-ahead. "Firing room. We have main engine start," he noted.

Under the electric lights beneath a dark sky, the shuttles' engines fired simultaneously and rose, dumping a shimmering cloud bank on the runway as they reached for the stars.

Once they cleared the tower, Launch Control turned communications over to Houston, where they were getting it all on NASA-TV and closed circuit feeds throughout the space center.

"*Freedom, Independence*, you are looking strong," Clark said.

"Your thrust is maxed. Both shuttles are go for ET separation," a tech reported.

Truman turned to Quincy, feeling better now that they were under way. "One down."

Sharp's voice broke in over the radio. "Initiating roll maneuver. We have SRB sep, over." It was confirmation that both orbiters had shed their twin solid rocket boosters. The reusable canisters fell away under parasol chutes, to be picked up in the Atlantic.

The orbiters screamed off against the drag of gravity in a struggle for altitude. Fifty miles above the cape they shot free of the atmosphere—the sky color in the windows plunged from bright blue to black, and stars powdered the heavens. The dour moon loomed over them. White sunlight flared on their wings.

Not that anyone on the orbiters was too preoccupied with soaking in the scenery—the first hard G-Forces were ramming them into their chair backs.

Clark's bland comment crackled over the radio: "Lookin' real good here, *Freedom*."

LCC had scheduled liftoff to intersect with the Russian Space Station's routine approach over the Atlantic. Launched by the Soviets in 1986, the space station had become the backbone of the International Space Station effort. Constructed of Russian and U.S.–made modules built on Earth and added on over a ten-year period, the continuously manned station served as an Earth observatory, zero-gravity lab, and acid test on international cooperation.

On the outside, much of the Russian Space Station's one-hundred-square-foot size was in her energy-collecting "sails"—large solar panels that converted light to the electricity that ran everything from onboard computers to electric shavers.

Inside, she was more than ever like a typical sailing yacht—cramped, lacking amenities, and wildly popular with out-of-town guests. Her continuous occupants were Russian cosmonauts—two or three, usually. Americans tended to come and go on shuttle sortie missions hauling cargo and cosmonauts on rotation duty. U.S. astronauts who stayed could count on the layover for the next connecting flight to last several months.

Working alone in one tunnel of the complex was Russian cosmonaut Lev Andropov. For the time being, he had an unusual luxury—the entire space station to himself. Not counting the several million amoebae in the lab, of course. Andropov had recently caught himself talking with them—it had been some time since he'd had a visitor.

On this particular day, Andropov's current project, like the one before it and all the ones before that, was a repair job. In the circumlocution of a milcrat (military bureaucrat), the Russian was employing a forged metal striker to apply mechanical assistance to an optical signal console. This was otherwise known as hitting a video monitor with a hammer.

Like any good spaceman, Andropov took pride in his ability to fly not just according to the rule book but by the seat of his pants. It was the one thing nobody could teach you, the way you left your mark. And sometimes, it was the way you stayed alive.

At last Andropov coaxed a signal from the monitor and allowed himself a recreational thought about the American asteroid team he awaited. Their futile, ridiculous mission was clearly symptomatic of an education system based on television entertainment and comic books. He refused to dwell on it. On to the next repair.

Andropov's isolation in the space station had bred in him a detachment that had soured, making him aloof and irritable. His reports to RSA (the Russian Space Agency) had grown rigidly brief and to the point, and he'd disconnected the station entirely from the drone of ham operator calls originating primarily in the United States.

He spent day after day with the silent machinery—nursing, prodding, patching, mending, replacing, refurbishing...playing a twenty-first-century version of Hercules battling the many-headed hydra of a to-do list.

———————

Freedom and *Independence* were in barbecue mode— taking a slow roll for thermal conditioning on the way to the space station. As the ships turned, the flight deck windows showed them a scene of bright blue atmosphere followed by the black void of space. Radio chatter washed over everything, describing each and every small action at the controls on *Freedom*, on *Independence*, in Houston; punctuated by a comment, a joke, a comment on a comment, layers upon layers...

Then they were there.

Short bursts from the orbital maneuvering systems in the nose of each ship and from twin pods aft of the payload bays brought them alongside. The payload bays opened to give the airlock modules on the space station access to the crew cabin bulkhead.

"Initiate docking beacon," Davis radioed from *Independence*.

Tucker performed the detail and confirmed it. "Docking beacon engaged."

Sharp and Watts followed the same procedure on *Freedom*, prepping for the connection to the T-shaped twin docking ports on opposite sides of the station.

The momentum from the American spaceships had a rotisserie effect on the docking station. "Russian space station's fired her rockets," Sharp explained. "This'll give her enough spin to simulate gravity and let us work faster—but it'll also make you queasy, so prepare yourself."

"Yeah, it's about time—I haven't thrown up in almost an hour," Rockhound said sarcastically, giving the pilot the full benefit of his opinion.

Sharp ignored it. "Fuel teams prepare to unload," he ordered.

Green lights signaled depressurization, and the airlocks opened onto the space station. The *Freedom* team—Harry, Sharp, Gruber, and Rockhound—entered from one side. From the other side, out of the *Independence*, came A. J., Davis, Tucker, and Oscar.

As they entered, Andropov appeared in the passage and hung there, batlike, upside down. His dark eyes and grave expression made the Americans feel like trespassers.

"Welcome to my domain," he said somberly. "Who is in charge of you?"

Colonel Sharp identified himself. Then, "We should start the O-2 transfer immediately," he said. Time was critical; he was ready to start loxing—fueling *Freedom* and *Independence* with liquid oxygen—without further ado.

The cosmonaut's reply was nonchalant. "You realize this plan . . . for breaking asteroid into two perfect pieces . . . is not possible," he commented.

Sharp's expression showed he had neither the

time nor the inclination to debate the issue. "We only have a thirty-five-minute window," he noted.

"I am not gas station," the cosmonaut reminded them sharply. "This is laboratory. I am here alone— in charge of important and outstanding scientific experiments. So. Do not be touching any one thing. Is this understood by everybody?"

It was frustrating. In less than a week Earth was toast and this guy was primarily concerned about their watching out for his toys.

"Got it," said Sharp, humoring him.

"Good," said Andropov, grim-faced.

Suddenly the Russian collapsed to the floor. "Bitch!" Angry and embarrassed, he struggled to get up. "Space legs!" Long-term habitation in a zero-G environment tended to cause body fluids to rise from the extremities, weakening the legs' ability to support weight even at the low level of sim-gravity on the space station.

"Happens to everybody!" the Russian brushed off. In case the Americans were under the wrong impression that zero-G illnesses were endemic to Russians.

Harry offered him a hand, but the cosmonaut chose to get up on his own. "I do it," he said, further making the point. Then he straightened himself uncertainly and wobbled off, expecting them to follow.

A. J. turned to Sharp. "You know what I like about that guy? His personality," he said lightly.

The corridors inside the space station were cramped and claustrophobic, with pipes and tubing that reminded Harry of an old sub.

When they neared the fuel storage area, Andropov halted them for a wardrobe change. To save energy, the fuel storage pod was now treated as crew quarters. From a metal locker he withdrew the heavy cold suit needed to enter and passed it to A. J.

"You will be observing pressure gauge," Andropov told him.

Without thinking about it too much, Chick poked a finger over a nondescript object at the top of a full, open storage bin, and the Russian rushed to him. "When I say touch nothing, I am not joke-making!" he shouted.

"I'm sorry, I was just—" Chick tried to explain.

The Russian cut him off with an explanation of his own. "If something break," he told Chick earnestly, "Russian Space Agency make me pay for it."

Chick shook his head. Unbelievable. *But, hey, Andropov,* he thought, *put this in your pipe and smoke it*—"If this split-the-asteroid plan is not gonna work, as you say," Chick reminded him, "then it doesn't really matter, does it?"

"You are not as funny as you believe you are," said the Russian, making a final adjustment to his own cold suit.

———————

The passageway to the fuel storage area was a twenty-five-foot shaft—it was like taking the sewer line. No thought had been given to heating the fuel pod—there was little human traffic, and saving energy was always a consideration on the space station, even in the full face of the sun. They'd learned the hard way in 1996, when a space station pod carrying garbage played bumper tag with the solar panels on the Skylar unit that supplied fifty percent of the station's solar power, leading to a series of blackouts and computer failures.

A. J. followed Lev through the fuel storage section to a differential pressure gauge that measured the variance in the fuel line between the supply side—the storage tanks—and the intakes—the "gas tanks" in the orbiters' cargo bays.

"See gauge?" the cosmonaut said to him. "You watch. One-fifty? Good. One-sixty? Okay. Two hundred? Very bad. Disaster for space station." A break along the line could set off any number of problems. Outside the space station, a ruptured gas line could become a kind of quickie thruster, like punching the gas pedal without the benefit of steering. A break inside, the Russian didn't want to think about it.

"You tell Lev if before very bad," he cautioned A. J.

"What's *Lev?*" A. J. said.

"Lev is me," Andropov told him. "Colonel Lev Andropov." He was surprised A. J. was unfamiliar with his name.

"Back home I am a hero," he mentioned.

"I'm not arguing with you," said A. J.

Back to the question of the valve. "If past two hundred? You hit shut-off valve. Here." He showed

A. J. the chicken switch, a nondescript steel handle, then headed out.

On the deck over the fuel storage area, the American teams worked feverishly to set up the transfer of fuel into the shuttles.

After a few minutes' setup, the fuel transfer was under way. LOX (liquid oxygen at minus 400 degrees Fahrenheit) was pumping through a liquid propellant transfer hose that ran through the docking port to an interior propellant intake valve in the payload bay of the orbiters. As the gas cooled, the line in the heated personnel area of the station developed condensation.

"How long have you been up here—alone?" Rockhound asked Andropov.

"Eighteen months," he answered.

"That is a long-ass time," Rockhound commiserated.

"It was supposed to be for only ninety days," Andropov said. "So yes. I am lonely alone a lot by myself." It was about as personal as Andropov got. Waiting on a weather window in Cocoa Beach prior to his shuttle connection, Andropov had channel-surfed some American daytime television—soap operas, primarily. From this he'd formed the opinion that the United States was in general a nation of touchy-feelies.

"I'd like to take this opportunity to say that I'm sorry for all the upheaval in your country. It must be hard," Oscar said.

Proving Lev's point. The Russian just looked at him, deadpan. The kid had no idea.

Down below, A. J. watched the pressure start to rise. "Hey, Lev?" he mentioned. "Pressure's climbing. . . ."

Oscar's comment had distracted him. Must be hard? Lev was thinking. "My father was from Mordovinia," he told Oscar. "You know Mordovinia? It once had largest bomb factory in all of Soviet Union. He assembled impact sensors. He loved his job. Today in Mordovinia, they make key chains. Now they have to be proud of building key chains."

Oscar had to figure that really was kind of a letdown.

Andropov's comment about the key-chain factory made Rockhound wonder how much of this Russian-built spaceship they were cruising on represented the handiwork of disgruntled ex-Soviet factory laborers. "We're gonna die in this piece of shit," he concluded.

Andropov turned on him. "This piece of shit, as you have called it, has lasted double time what Americans thought!" he growled. "Why? Because of great Russian technology is why! It will even outlive Earth, huh? Isn't that great irony? And if you are not successful with asteroid, when my family is dead, I promise, you are the man I will blame," Andropov said bitterly, giving them a glimpse of the emotional load he was under.

"Christ, is there a Russian phrase for *lighten up?*" Rockhound grumbled.

Watts broke in. "Check your hoses, we've got some thermal variation—check your pressure buildup," she warned.

Andropov turned to her, softening. "You are first woman I have seen in more than one year...." Then he spotted the problem. "*Leeeeeaaaaaak! Get out! Out! Out!*" he screamed. They were all disappearing in the fog of the fuel leak inside the space station.

"Christ! E-vac! E-vac! Prepare to unhook shuttles! *Move!*" Sharp barked.

"This sucks!" A. J. noted. "What the hell happened, Lev? I was calling you!" he complained.

"So you turn off!" Lev urged. "Pull lever!"

"*This is the lever!*" A. J. showed him the piece of metal that had snapped off in his grasp.

"They say don't fly on Russian airplanes," Rockhound observed dryly. "We should've seen this coming."

"Not heated, minus one hundred," the Russian thought aloud. Then to the others, "Hold breath or lungs freeze! And touch nothing."

Davis was fumbling around in the dense vapor. "Where the hell are they?"

"Get in the damned cabin!" Sharp yelled. He was shoving astronauts through the airlock to the *Freedom.* "Did we get all the O-2?" he wanted to know from Watts. The fuel was an absolute must.

"Affirmative! Let's push off!" Watts cried.

Harry balked. Push off? Were they fucking crazy? "We've gotta make sure they got back!" he yelled, meaning the other team.

"There's no time!" Sharp insisted.

"Where's A. J.?" Harry yelled.

"Get inside before this thing rips apart!" Sharp argued. He grabbed Harry. To Watts: "Shut the doors and fire her up!"

Harry pulled away. "They're still out there!" he yelled.

"It's them or *all of us! This is an order!*" Watts screamed.

"We have to *go now!*" Tucker agreed.

"Full thrusters!" Sharp ordered.

And as the Freedom pulled away, the station exploded into a fireball. Shrapnel narrowly missed the shuttle as it sped off toward the moon.

CHAPTER TWELVE

"That is why I asked you to touch nothing," Lev admonished A. J. They were looking at the broken handle of the shut-off valve in A. J.'s hand.

"You might wanna talk to the boys in the lever department about that," A. J. suggested, handing it over. At least they'd made it through the airlock onto the *Independence*.

Davis radioed the news to the *Freedom*. "The entire *Independence* crew is accounted for—we're even heavy one cosmonaut. How about you?"

Watts breathed relief. "We're all in one piece, *Independence*. Glad to hear you're still up and running."

Behind her, Chick was reviewing his life, the choices he'd made, with Harry. Looking out the window at Earth, he reminded his friend, "I followed you all over that thing. And now I've followed you up here."

Harry nodded, a little wistfully.

Chick continued, "I must not be very smart. . . ."

Harry frowned. "Look at that." He pointed, gesturing at the blue planet in the window again. "Just floating there. All those people living on that ball . . . it's almost impossible, isn't it? That right now . . . they're all down there. . . . Even kids too young to know what's going on . . . their lives are in your hands. Mine."

Harry turned away, catching a glimpse of his personal effects, his Bible. He opened it and rested his eyes on a photograph kept inside. An old photograph of himself as a younger man, with his daughter Grace.

"If I keep thinking that way, I'll lose my mind." He shuddered.

Rockhound's mood was introspective as well. "I've been doing this mental inventory of the things I love," he told them. "My fondest memories. Categorizing them, you know? 'Cause if this all goes south, I think it's probably a good thing to die with your fondest memories coursing through your brain . . . in case there is, you know, something beyond. . . ."

Chick was almost afraid to ask. "So what's your fondest memory, Rockhound?"

"Well, Chickie, I'd love to tell you it's something magical, like my mother's loving hugs. Or havin' a catch with the old man. Or the first time I saw Venice."

"But . . . ?" The suspense was killing Max, sort of.

"Shit," Rockhound confessed. "It's Jackie Bisset in *The Deep*. Smuggling raisins in that wet T-shirt—

okay, sue me! But that's a goddamned reason to believe!"

There it was, straight from the heart. Tiny and shriveled up and as hard as a rock, maybe, but a heart nonetheless.

Oscar was unwrapping slightly. "Guess what!" he told them. "I don't want to go back! I swear, I'm a bundle of nerves on Earth; I mean, I don't know if it's the whole weightless stuff or what, but mentally I feel weightless, ya know? I can think up here!"

He was beginning to sound like the membership director for Cults Unlimited.

———

The *Independence* followed the *Freedom* toward the rough, shadowy mountain ranges on the face of the huge white orb that was the moon. Beyond it, the asteroid was barely visible in the distance.

The asteroid——it was a huge, craggy mass surrounded on all sides by a debris cluster of rock and ice, the ice glinting on and off in reflected sunlight, like a bunch of brilliant fireflies.

"We have visual of the target, Houston. Velocity thirty-three hundred miles an hour," Sharp reported.

On both orbiters the crews buckled into their seat restraints and harnesses.

The face of the moon filled their field of vision forward.

"We've lost visual contact with the target, Houston," Sharp noted.

The spaceships closed in on the dark-side horizon of the moon, swinging around it on the gravitation pull.

"Sixty-four seconds on the mark," Watts said, counting down.

"Eighteen seconds to radio interrupt," came from Houston.

"Booster sequence confirm," said Sharp.

"Rockets ready. On your mark," Watts responded.

Truman's voice crackled over the radio, "See you on the other side," and clicked out.

———

A pall hung over Houston Communications. "Radio contact terminated. We're out," Clark said.

"Nine and a half Gs for eleven minutes," Truman said. The force on the shuttle teams would be enormous. "I'd start praying right around now."

Kimsey was curious. "Anyone ever done that before?"

"Yeah," Truman said. "Vlad the Russian monkey back in '56. We'll pick 'em up again in sixteen minutes."

"If they're still alive," Clark said gloomily.

———

The G-forces rammed the space travelers into their seats, their arms picked up three hundred pounds, immovable, and a weight like a steamroller went over their chests, no—parked there, crushing them. Breathing, staying conscious—both were impossible.

"Fourteen   thousand...sixteen   thousand... twenty-two thousand miles an hour," Watts croaked through clenched teeth. Then she blacked out.

CHAPTER THIRTEEN

A voice was heard on *Freedom*——Clark on the radio. "This is Houston. Come in, *Freedom*, come in, *Independence*."

Sharp came back to him on the radio. The message was broken, full of static in Houston, but Sharp figured they were overjoyed.

Good thing Houston didn't have pictures.

Sharp's message was just, "You've gotta see this to believe it." Then, "God*damn*, we've got debris!"

"What is it?" Clark said from Houston.

"Asteroid junk! Severe turbulence!" Sharp exclaimed.

When the orbiters rounded the moon, they found themselves in the shotgun spray of the debris field roaring ahead of the asteroid——a bomb-blast cloud of rock-and-ice-throwing bergs as big as houses that flashed in the sunlight and boulders that pulverized the lunar surface, ricocheting off.

Harry did a quick mental calculation. He figured

they had about a fifty percent chance of getting demolished by a rock. The other fifty percent said they'd get demolished by an iceberg.

"It's bad here, Colonel! We should peel off! Try again!" Tucker pleaded. They went through a hailstorm of rock and ice. Then it cleared, but it came back with a vengeance.

From the *Independence*, Davis radioed an AMF— Adios, Mother Fucker. "*We're hit! We've lost thruster control! Mayday! Mayday! We're not going to make it! We're going down!*"

The *Independence* was handling like a tin can behind a honeymoon car. She end-over-ended above the *Freedom*, spraying blue flame from a rear thruster. Sharp nose-dived, swung away, then zigzagged around an incoming iceberg. "Everyone go to life support!" Davis shouted.

"*Mayday, Houston . . . mayday! . . .*" Tucker blared. Behind him, Noonan freaked and bolted for the safety emergency hatch's explosive release charges.

"Get away from that door!" Tucker yelled at him.

"I ain't dyin' on this thing!" Noonan cried.

A rock smashed through the windshield, gouging into Tucker. The cabin pressure blew, and the vacuum of space sucked him and Davis violently out the window. Noonan blew the hatch and exploded into the void. The big pop in the cabin ruptured the bulwark to the cargo bay and blew heavy equipment out the holes in the nose like a blast from a shotgun.

It all occurred without sound, like some horrific, unstoppable silent movie.

Then the ship skidded down on the asteroid, shredding her fuselage, gutting herself over a saw-tooth boulder field.

The bodies of A. J. and Lev were thrown around like rag dolls in the rear cabin.

———————

SLAP! In the pressurized cabin of the *Freedom*, Sharp and Watts recoiled as Davis's body pummeled off the windshield, followed by the din of pipes and heavy drilling equipment.

Harry, Sharp, Watts, and the crew of *Freedom* stared at the radio in shock. Nothing came from *Independence* except static.

Houston knew. *Independence*'s systems monitors had flashed off: Pressurization, zero, cabin oxygen, zero. "System-wide failure..."

The future didn't look any more promising for *Freedom*. She was past the debris cloud at the asteroid's leading edge, but the asteroid surface had so many rock and boulder features that it looked like an immense cemetery. "Houston!" Sharp yelled. "We lost our landing field!"

"We're coming in too hot!" Watts warned.

Sharp fired the thrusters, trying to regain control. The ship came into the scree sideways, slinging gravel and ice chunks.

Then it stopped.

Sharp broke the silence. "Cabin status? Anyone hurt?" He turned around and saw one of the crew wearing a bloody gash across the forehead. "Gruber! You okay?"

"Just fine."

Harry was checking, too. "You guys good?" Chick and Max both gave him the thumbs up.

The *Freedom* had lights, at least—flickering, but they were there.

"Initiate system-wide system check," Sharp ordered. "Make sure we can still get off this rock."

In Houston, Clark was on the radio. "*Freedom*, come in. *Freedom*."

Nothing.

"*Independence*, this is Houston. Do you read?"

Truman looked around for Grace. He found her, staring at the edge of madness, living in a nightmare.

"Listen, you might not want to be here," he said to her.

"I don't have anywhere else to go," she said.

———

Watts went over the gauges. "Engine seals—check. Fuel seals—check. Pressure seals—check."

"So where's the other shuttle?" Rockhound wondered aloud.

"*Independence* is off the grid," Sharp told him.

"Off the grid?" Rockhound demanded. "What

are you, a freaking cyborg? What's that mean—off the grid?"

"You saw it. She's gone," Gruber said. Like a little kid, trying to make sense of things after a shock.

Harry was devastated. Thinking about A. J., the team . . . he gripped his Bible hard.

"Maybe if I'd read this thing, I'd know what to say, but I don't. God, watch over them. May they rest in peace."

Chick bowed his head. "Jesus Christ. This whole goddamned thing . . ."

"It could've been us," Harry told him. "Maybe it should've been. But we did make it. And now we're gonna deal with it."

Max was taking it hard. "This isn't happening," he groaned.

"*Max*," Harry said firmly. "We've only got eight hours. Let's do this thing and get the hell outta here."

But the ones who really needed the pep talk were on the ground, in Houston. Clark announced that *Independence* was "flatlined, with total spectrum failure." No vital signs.

Truman looked pale. "Tell me we still have *Freedom*," he said.

"Pulse fragments," Skip said. "If they're alive, they're working on it."

It was a good guess. At that moment, Watts was swapping panels, and Sharp was punching in command chains, trying to bring the system back up. Rockhound was doing his part, staring at a video monitor and waiting for images from Earth to come on.

"We're not getting a damned thing on the internal nav system," Sharp complained. Without computer navigation they didn't need to leave—there was no place they could go.

"I know where we are," Rockhound pointed out.

Sharp's face tightened. "Get away from the equipment please." He checked an LCD gauge for radio signal power, and it was zero.

Watts had a thought. "I'm flipping the backup generator, but even with that, our comm signal's cut in half until we get back main power."

Rockhound said, "We're in segment 202, Lateral Grid Nine. Site 15H32, give or take a few yards. Captain America blew the landing by twenty-six miles."

Sharp bristled. "How the hell do you know that?"

"Because I'm a genius," Rockhound explained.

Watts was busy. "I can't read these gauges," she fretted. "They're all peaked, like we're plugged into some kind of magnetic field. . . ."

"Who on this spaceship wants to know why?" Rockhound said, mostly to Sharp. "The reason we were shooting for Grid Eight is that thermographics indicated that Grid Nine, our current parking space, was especially compressed iron ferrite. In astronaut-talk, that means you landed us on a goddamned iron plate."

Then he gave a Sharp one of his "thanks a lot"

looks. Poor bastard. It was tough being smarter than everybody else.

"Let's wheel out the remote satellite link," Sharp said. "We need that radio."

CHAPTER FOURTEEN

On the other side of a jagged range the wreck of the *Independence* lay upside down on a bed of rubble. Steam and frozen gases leaked from a hundred small ruptures. Deep within the wreckage, a dark shape swung over the ruins. Emergency lights flickered.

A. J.

Hanging from his harness, upside down, he was alive and thinking, *Who else?*

Halsey was wasted.

Noonan—gone.

Oscar, too.

What about Bear? Bear was okay, wasn't he?

Bear was still hanging in his harness like A. J.—*safety belts save lives*—only with a boot jammed into some kind of grillwork.

A. J. disengaged himself from his safety equipment and made his way over there.

"You've gotta help me do this," he told Bear,

wondering how he was ever going to get the man's foot out of the trap.

"No sweat," Bear croaked. "What do you need?" Always willing to lend a hand.

Then he passed out.

Down the passageway, somebody was swearing in Russian. Andropov appeared in the cabin, out of breath and shaken.

"Where are the rest?" Andropov sighed. But he already knew. They were dead.

"Lucky ... they are very lucky...." the Russian uttered. His eyes were wet.

A. J. lifted himself onto an Armadillo surface explorer. "Okay, I've got a reading here," he said, tapping at the controls. "This is what we're gonna do: We're gonna get in the Armadillo, and we're gonna find Harry and the other shuttle."

Andropov looked dubious. "And why then are you so optimistic the other team is not dead?" he wondered.

"Well, that's just the difference between you and me." A. J. shrugged. "Help me with Bear, will you?"

Rockhound and Harry were suited up, out on the surface. The scene was tranquil and bizarre. They were in a small, dark valley under the watchful flood-light of the moon.

"We're in space, Harry," Rockhound gasped. "Holy shit..."

Harry was busy. He'd selected a drill site. Make a hole, drop in a bomb. "We'll sightsee later," he said. "This iron can't be more than fifty feet deep."

"How do you figure that?" Rockhound wanted to know.

Simple, Harry thought. "I figure if it is more than fifty feet, we're screwed."

An Armadillo rolled down the ramp from the cargo bay. It was Max and Chick, with the drilling tools. They stopped and set up the arm, the transmission, the bit....

"Just another day makin' a hole," Max was singing, "in outer friggin' space...."

The bit turned, lowered, and bit into the rock. Harry and Chick took turns angling it against the walls of the drill hole. Then—

"What the hell—?" Harry said.

Without warning, the bit had broken and the drive was dead. Harry was horrified, Max pale and staring.

"Harry?" Max said. "Did you see that?"

"Well," Rockhound scoffed. "This is a goddamned Greek tragedy...."

Harry shook it off. "We've all seen bits get fried before," he said.

"Not after ten feet," Chick said.

"Well, now we have!" Harry insisted. "Get that look off your face! Bring out the Deliverance. Let's re-bit this as fast as we can. Move!"

"Houston, this . . . *reedom* . . . do . . . ou read?" came through the static. ". . . *Freedom* . . . do you read? Radio source coordinates approximate site location 15H32 . . ."

Watts was coming through to Houston!

The control room erupted in cheers and applause. Grace laughed.

"*Freedom!*" Truman cheered. "Yes! God bless *Freedom!*"

"What's your current status?" Clark asked.

Sharp gave them a summary. "Shuttle flight capability not yet known—we're also having electric and antenna difficulties, but we have commenced drilling." A minor triumph.

Rockhound and Max clamped in the new bit, and Harry put his hand on the drive switch. "All right, let's go to twenty-five!" he said. Warning them to stay clear—

The Deliverance, their big bit, scored the rock. The blade angled in, a ragged spiral of rock twisted out of the hole like a vine, then everything froze— the bit chewed, jammed in the rock.

"Harry——" Rockhound started in.

"Shut up," Harry told him. "We're cutting

through a plate. Some are tougher than others, you know that. Let's get another bit on this thing. Iron Maiden. Let's go!" Piece of cake.

———————

Truman, Kimsey, and a gang of NASA and military techs were watching another disaster develop on a computer graphics monitor.

"Before the asteroid passed the moon, her rotation was stable at thirty-two degrees on an X axis," a NASA tech pointed out. "But now look—the lunar gravity's put her in a spin. She's rolling on all three axes. This wasn't expected, sir—"

Truman scowled. "What does this mean for communications?"

"Not good," the tech confirmed. "We'll have definite contact with the shuttle for only seven more minutes. After that, it's radio darkness."

"For how long?"

The tech shook his head. "Can't predict the asteroid's position—we'll lose contact a minimum of ninety seconds. And a maximum of . . . forever, sir."

Kimsey turned to a nuke tech. "If they lose shuttle comm, when do we lose the nuke?"

"The weapon remote receives its signal from a Milstar satellite, sir—different orbit, higher powered frequency—if we've got the shuttle for seven minutes, we have a remote detonation capability for an additional five." A bank shot, in other words.

Get ready to pull the trigger, Kimsey thought. Now. "Get me the President right away."

CHAPTER FIFTEEN

On the *Independence*, Bear lowered himself into Armadillo Two. The pain was agonizing.

They were all trapped in the cargo bay. "Look how good your American shuttle made safe landing," Lev pointed out.

Sweet guy. A. J. was ready to throttle him. "Listen. It's not my shuttle, okay? I'm not even an astronaut. I'm an oil driller. I shouldn't even be here."

"Really." The Russian never let up. "So what are you doing—" He broke off halfway through the insult, genuinely surprised. "What are you doing, A. J.?"

"I'm getting us out of here," A. J. told him matter-of-factly. He crawled high on the Armadillo and pulled the jacket off the cannon.

"You might want to get down for this, Lev," he mentioned.

Lev scrambled into the Armadillo as A. J. sighted down the barrel and started throwing toggle switches.

BLAM! The cannon bucked and blew an opening through the metal shuttle skin.

On the asteroid surface, Harry, Rockhound, and Chick watched the slow progress of the new bit against the rock. Harry checked his watch.

"We're way behind," he said. To Max in the Armadillo he said, "I need some action down there. I want you to wind it out. Gimme fourth gear all the way."

Max double-checked the temp gauge. "Boss, we're running hot already."

"Do it or I'll come in and do it for you," Harry shot back.

Max punched the clutch, and the Armadillo shuddered. At the business end of the drive arm, the bit blurred, raced for several seconds, and then lost power, dropping down to low speed—the gearbox was out! "What's up with the tranny?" Harry demanded.

"The good news is at least we've got first gear left," Max told him. It was slow or no go.

Suddenly they were peppered with a shotgun blast of shrapnel—the whole transmission had burst right through the housing. Flying bits and pieces were scattered around them.

"*Shit!*" Chick yelled.

A hard gust of wind hit them, followed by another one, harder. As if the asteroid were fighting back.

Harry hung on. "You want to make this tough? Okay. We can do it tough." He glared at the rock. "I've got another transmission inside, and I'm coming, so bring it on, bitch."

Meanwhile Sharp and Gruber were trying to lock down the remote antennae. In the windstorm atmosphere of the asteroid, it wasn't easy. Harry's voice sounded in Sharp's earphones. "Sharp, we need some help."

Sharp paused. "What happened?"

"Meet me in the shuttle."

In *Freedom's* cockpit, Watts worked the electrical lines. More lights came alive. She thought about Mission Control, wondered how much of this they were getting on the video monitors.

Sharp and Harry were back.

"What's the situation?" Sharp wanted to know.

Harry frowned. "I'm drillin' into something I shouldn't be—this thing just ate two drill bits faster than I've ever seen. Now it's killed our transmission."

"So how deep are we?"

Don't ask. "I need your help in the cargo—"

"There's an assessment report due now," Sharp insisted. "We're supposed to be at two hundred feet. So, how deep are we?"

"Not as deep as we will be when you stop asking questions that waste my time," Harry growled.

"I need a depth to report."

Don't ask me that. "What's important is that you help us get that transmission on—"

"I'll decide what's important!" Sharp barked. "My job, my responsibility is to supervise and report! We've got eight hundred feet to drill, you've had two and a half hours—where are we?"

"Fifty-seven feet!" Harry yelled back.

Sharp was stunned. That was all? He headed for the cockpit radio.

Harry yelled after him. "We landed on goddamned steel—once we get through the metal plate, it'll go as fast as any other job!"

He hoped.

Sharp picked up a drilling timetable card and went on radio and video transmission to Houston.

Harry shouldered past Watts and ripped the card from Sharp's hand.

Sharp kept going on the radio, "Transmission change twenty minutes, puts drilling final at ten hours—that's four hours past Zero Barrier!"

Harry grabbed the transmitter. "This is the way drillin' goes sometimes! You don't know what you're gonna hit till you hit it, so you can't panic 'cause we had a few bad innings—" Telling them to keep the faith, not knowing how much of it was getting through the static and video flutter.

He turned to Sharp. "Now I need you back in the cargo bay to help drag that thing out here."

Sharp looked beat. "Just face it. You can't do it. You just can't. I knew from the beginning bringing you and your crew along to do this job was the biggest goddamned mistake in NASA histor——"

Harry's arm shoved Sharp's face into the video tap, putting him up on all the monitors in Houston.

Sharp lashed at him and broke away.

Harry glared at him. "You stay here. Supervise and report. I'll do the work." And he turned and went after the tranny.

————

At Mission Control, the techs tried to hold sound and a picture. What were they *doing* up there?

Kimsey answered a red phone. "Yes. Yessir. We saw that, too. Yessir, very difficult, but perhaps we should wait unt——"

He listened, and his face tightened.

"Yessir. I understand."

He hung up and turned to Truman. "Dan, get them out of there. E-vac right now."

Truman didn't get it. "What are you doing?"

"I've been ordered to override the system," Kimsey said.

A crew of Marines entered the room, shielding a pair of military aides carrying a Nuclear Command Link suitcase. The detonator.

"What is this?" Truman said.

Kimsey had orders. "Secondary protocol. The President and his advisers feel the drilling isn't working, and we're about to lose radio contact, maybe for good. We only have a few more minutes with guaranteed ability to remote-detonate that nuke. If we don't do it now we lose control—"

Truman had had enough. "You should tell the President that A: He must immediately fire his advisers, and B: If we blow that nuke on the surface, we're wasting a perfectly good bomb and blowing our one chance at doing this right!"

It was out of Kimsey's hands. "His mind is made up."

Truman wasn't having any of it. "So is mine! General, you cannot do this!"

"It isn't my call," Kimsey told him. "It isn't yours. My Commander in Chief, the President of the United States, has made a decision. Get them out of there now."

Truman balked. "We can't reach them! We don't even know if that shuttle can fly yet!" He jerked the receiver off the cradle of the red phone....

———

Patiently, silently, Gruber on the asteroid continued to lock down the remote antenna....

———

"Mr. President!" Truman shouted. "My point is simple: You do this, you kill me, you kill you, you kill the First Lady...."

Truman stopped a beat, then held the phone out to Kimsey. "He wants you."

Kimsey took the phone. "Yessir. Yessir. I understand." Then he hung up. "The President's advisers believe there's a shot that a surface detonation will slow down the asteroid enough to miss the planet."

Truman was disgusted. "I've shown you Quincy's numbers—that won't slow it down enough!"

"Well," Kimsey argued, "it's better than doing nothing, which is what you've got right now!"

A NASA tech added some icing to the cake. "We still can't get through to 'em—"

"*Keep trying!*" Truman barked.

"The order for remote detonation," Kimsey said, "is in thirty seconds." He put his key in the link.

Grace shuddered. "But you haven't even told them yet!" The shuttle team! "You can't do that!" she screamed. "*That's my father up there!*" Two soldiers held her back.

Truman kept working on him. "There's still time to do this right! *This is one order you should not follow, and you fucking know it!*" he shouted.

But the aides put their keys in the detonator and turned them—

Click.

Click.

Kimsey's turn.

———————

Click.

———————

Rockhound and Max had the transmission off the drive. In the cargo bay of the orbiter, Harry and Chick struggled to guide the new large appliance out of storage.

"I've got it."

"Keep going."

They had her almost past the big nine-foot nuke when Chick noticed the clock on the damned thing. "Look, it's ticking."

Harry made a face. That wasn't right. Four minutes . . . 3:59 . . . 3:58 . . .

CHAPTER SIXTEEN

"*Sharp! Get back here!*" Harry yelled.

Sharp appeared in the bay.

Harry's eyes told him to look at the bomb clock. He watched for a reaction.

Basically, Sharp lost his shit.

"*Watts!*" Sharp screamed. "*Get the shuttle ready to e-vac in two minutes, now!*"

"What's happening?" Harry wanted to know. Was there a problem?

"*Secondary protocol!*" Sharp bellowed.

"What's secondary protocol?" Harry asked him. Must be bad. Watts was losing her shit, too.

"I don't know if we can fire up in time!" Watts yelled.

Harry was getting impatient. "What the hell is secondary protocol?" he insisted.

Sharp was manhandling the bomb. Trying to dance it out of there. Harry and Chick automatically gave him a hand—

"They're detonating this thing from Earth! We've gotta drop it and go!"

—bearhugging the thing. *Did he say detonate?* Harry thought.

"Max! Rockhound!" Harry barked into his headset. "Double-time it back to the shuttle!"

No way they could make it.

"I've got a man out there, too!" Sharp yelled. "There's no time!"

Harry grabbed Sharp hard. "Without putting this bomb down eight hundred feet into a fault line, blowing it up's just a real expensive fireworks show! Now, they might not think we can drill it, but I do."

Sharp's face had no color. "The order to detonate could only have come from the President of the United States—"

Harry: "Well, guess what. I never voted for the wimp! We can do this right. Turn the bomb off!"

In the flight deck cockpit, Watts coaxed something out of the control panel—a blink of light. Not enough power. "Central generator's not coming back online, Sharp!" she reported. "We are not going to make it!"

Sharp and Harry were struggling against each other in the bay. Harry twisted away and drew a wrench—ready to smash the damned clock.

Sharp pulled a handgun on him. "Don't!" he ordered. "You could set it off!"

"Then you do it!" Harry shouted. "Stop the clock so we can do our job!"

Sharp flipped out. "I'm under orders to protect a surface detonation!"

———

Mission Control looked like halftime in the loser's locker room. Only one guy still thought they had a chance: Truman.

Holding out for a miracle—

—He saw the bomb control panel countdown freeze and flash *OVERRIDE SUCCESSFUL.*

No boom.

Kimsey couldn't believe it. "Do it again," he told one of the Marines.

The soldier moved to a computer and slid the attending technician back in his chair. Then he shut off the console.

———

The clock on the nuke went dead at 1:09.

Harry had a pair of pipe tongs. He lunged at Sharp with them, clamping his neck. Wanting to pop his helmet like a champagne cork . . .

But first, Harry thought, *I would like to make the following editorial comment:* "Figures, doesn't it?" he roared. "President can never make up his mind about *anything!*"

Sharp croaked. "It could start up again—"

"Which is why," Harry explained firmly, letting up a bit on the mechanical headlock, "you're gonna take apart that bomb right now! I don't want any more surprises!"

Wishful thinking. A Marine at Mission Control thought he had the detonator signal working again. Watts in the shuttle thought she had the central generator up again, too.

"We're coming back online!" Watts yelled. "We have full power!" *Freedom* was working again!

Unfortunately, so was timer on the bomb.

1:08 . . .

Harry tightened the tongs around Sharp's neck.

1:07 . . .

"What *are* you?" he begged Sharp. "A goddamned computer? Bullshit! Right now you can follow an order, or you can do the right thing. And no matter what the hell they're saying down there, you're the man who's up here—you're the leader—and you can see something they can't! The better way! Sharp, this is the biggest risk anyone's ever had to take, but I've cut through slop and fire and stone so hard it crumbled diamond bits and goddamnit, we're drilling this one! We can beat this thing!" Harry hoped he was listening. "Please."

"Swear you can do it," Sharp croaked. "Swear on your daughter's life—my family's—"

Their eyes were locked. "Swear to God," Harry promised.

"I just hope I can shut it off," Sharp said.

———————

Sharp popped the cover on the LED clock and dug into a bird's nest of multicolored wire, feeling around for something. There——a plug-in, about the size of a credit card. He yanked it.

———   ———

Sharp's handiwork appeared on a monitor at the military console in Houston. "Sir," a nuke tech reported, "the remote isn't receiving our signal anymore."

Kimsey broke out in a cold sweat. "Have we lost the radio contact for good?"

"No, sir . . ." the tech responded.

Harry's voice broke through the expectant silence. "Houston, *you* have a problem. You see, I promised my daughter I'm coming home! No, I don't know what you are doing down there, but we've got a hole to dig up here."

Grace and Truman shared a look.

Kimsey closed his eyes. "Get me the President," he said.

CHAPTER SEVENTEEN

The sun was just creeping over the asteroid's horizon, illuminating a three-spired ridge, putting on a show for A. J., Bear, and Lev in the Armadillo.

"I never thought I'd be in a place as bad as Outer Mongolia," A. J. commented. He curved the heavy armored vehicle around a swimming-pool-sized pothole.

"Just thinking the same thing," Bear groaned. The jostling vehicle wasn't helping the pain he was still feeling from the crash.

A. J. laughed at his memory of Outer Mongolia. "Remember that? My second job, and Harry drops me in Outer Mongolia. That was hell."

Lev knew that place. "You think Outer Mongolia is bad? You should try Siberia. So cold that piss freezes immediately after pissing. Hurts."

A. J. pulled the Armadillo to a stop. They had come to a ridge with a fifty-foot drop—no way they could get down in the Armadillo.

———

At the drill site, Harry, Sharp, and Gruber were toiling with the new transmission. Behind them, the gun on the Armadillo swung jerkily, following the head movements of Rockhound, who was wearing its aiming helmet.

The area quaked with a subterranean shift.

"Is it me," Harry wondered, "or has it gotten twenty degrees hotter in the last ten minutes?"

Rockhound muttered, "The sun is hot... hot dogs are hot...."

Lying on his back under the Armadillo, Max strained to hold the lug straps tight against the transmission housing. "Okay," he said, "we're hot and heavy. Let her go."

Chick threw the go switch, and the drill bit went down in the pilot hole left by the last attempt.

"You know the job," Harry told them. "We've got two hours to rip through the plate and chew seven hundred feet! Let's make this one work!"

———

Lev struggled to find the English words to convey his bitter disappointment. "This is the worst situation ever. I'm telling you, you took the wrong road."

A. J. balked. "*Road?* What *road?* Is there some *map* you're not showing me?"

Lev shook his head. "I do not have pleasure being negative! Is this good for you?" Without thinking, A. J. picked up a stone and fired a fastball at the Russian. Lev ducked, and the rock sailed over him and sped away toward the horizon, like a feather on the wind.

A. J. brightened. "Ever heard of Evil Knievel?"

———————

The bit ground deep into the hard rock, then plunged.

"Harry!" Chick yelled. "Looking good! I think we broke through the plate!"

"Max, hang in there!" Harry relayed to the man at the throttle. "We're at one hundred fifty feet— keep it up, my man."

———————

A. J. clambered into the Armadillo and threw it in reverse. The heavy all-terrain tires spewed a low cloud of gravel that hung like a fog.

"Thrusters off when we make jump," Lev confirmed. "Thrusters on for to come down."

"This is going to work," A. J. said. "Say it."

Lev refused. "I am cynic. But if we make this . . . you will be hero like me."

A. J. gave it a thought. "That's fair." And he put the pedal to the metal with the cliff dead ahead. The Armadillo skipped off the edge, and A. J. cut the thrusters—they were cruising now. The vehicle shot across the jagged fissure and started to gain a little altitude.

Lev threw a thruster switch to guide them down. Nothing happened. Not even a spark.

"Bad," Lev remarked. "Bad—bad—this is very not good." He turned to A. J. "Jets not firing—we are floating to space!"

Then he headed for the air lock.

A. J. freaked. *"You're climbing outside?"*

Lev explained: *"I am saving your American ass!"*

"Go for it!" A. J. cheered. "This works, I'll keep you in Levis and Donna Summer records for life!"

Lev was already out, traversing the skin like a crab. The thruster port was caked with ice. Using a small torch, he tried to thaw out a valve. It sputtered—no good—and he moved the flame to the next one.

A. J. radioed further developments. "Lev! Incoming!" A flotilla of space rocks drifted in like flak, peppering the roof of the Armadillo. A side-mounted O-2 canister blew, scaring Lev onto the tow-winch cable.

The craft was end-over-ending like a bad pass. Desperate, A. J. punched a fire button, and the thruster blew, the burst sending them straight into a spire rising from the asteroid surface. The Armadillo dinged the wall, dragging Lev on the tow cable like a water-skier.

But they made it.

A. J.'s head popped out of the air lock. He eyed

Lev spread-eagled in the scree and clay and—look at that—the Russian was actually smiling.

"I must say," Lev said, "I am loving your macho confidence."

———————

At the same time, Truman was getting some happy news from a geo-tech at Mission Control: The asteroid was out of the moon's gravitational pull, and the asteroid's rotation was losing momentum. They were even restoring radio contact.

All good—"So why do you have that look on your face?" Truman wanted to know.

"Because I don't like those thermals—something's happening inside that rock, sir. Seismic activity has increased seven hundred percent in the past thirty minutes."

———————

At the drill site, stacks of pipe, tools, and drilling debris were accumulating. Harry and Sharp were wrestling pipe down the shaft while Rockhound watched their progress from a seat on the roof of the Armadillo.

His eyes unfocused, something on his mind...

"Give it a rest, guys," he mumbled. "I'll take care of it from here."

Then Rockhound pulled the cannon trigger, and the muzzle blasted wildly, sending everybody diving for cover. The gun turret followed Rockhound's movement as he searched for the team, blowing holes in the drilling area and just missing Harry and Gruber.

Harry charged the machine, clambered up, and tackled Rockhound to the ground.

"What the hell are you doing?" Harry yelled.

"Just shootin' a gun in space," Rockhound said simply. "What are you so testy about?"

He's snapped, Harry thought.

Meanwhile the bottom fell out of the pressure stability in the shaft—the needle fell like a stone on the console gauge inside the Armadillo.

A second later it jumped to maximum and plunged again, jumped, fell—

Quake.

The ground split and spiderwebbed like shattered glass under the men around the drill arm. Harry thought he saw the arm kick—just a few inches— or maybe not. That's what he wanted: not—

Again. That time it definitely kicked. "Pull the drill!" Harry shouted. "Max! Clear the hole now!"

Suddenly the surface trembled, and the ground felt fluid underfoot. Then it rocked like a steer and rattled the drill arm like a twig.

"*Get outta there!*" Harry bellowed. "Chick! Pull the pipe!"

Rockhound was oblivious. "It's the end of the world as we know it!" he sang wildly. "It's the end of the world as we know it, and I feel fiiiiiiiine!"

Harry fought the coupling between the Armadillo and the drill arm as the rig pounded and lurched from the streams of underground gas rushing out of the core and bursting at the surface. He pounded on the windshield—

"Max! Get outta there!"

But Chick grabbed him and pulled him away as the drilling hole blew, shooting pipe out of the ground like a missile silo. The concussion threw the Armadillo like a toy, sending Max into a panic. He punched the door lock without depressurizing. The vacuum outside sucked him like an egg out of the shell, sending him into orbit, gone.

"See you on the dark siiiiiiiide of the moon, Max!" Rockhound crowed.

The pipe, the drill arm, the Armadillo, a debris field of rock and machinery—and Max—vanished into the clear black sky.

On the shuttle, Clark's voice broke on the radio, "*Freedom*? Come in, *Freedom*. Request an update...."

Watts gave it to them flat out.

"Houston," she choked out, "this is *Freedom*. We just lost the Armadillo. Drilling... terminated. Unsuccessful."

The quake was over, too. The drill team stood like a gang of ghosts in the haze, and it was deathly quiet.

Except for Rockhound, who was completely unglued.

"Do you know the math that had to go into this? What are the odds that we'd end up here? Ya know, she doesn't even think she can start the shuttle! Guess what, guys! It's time to embrace the horror! We got front row seats to the end of the world, man! We're courtside! Let's ride it all the way in! It's a surfin' safari!"

Sharp and Gruber moved to the bomb.

CHAPTER EIGHTEEN

Kimsey watched the nuke techs working at the console to make contact with the bomb.

Truman approached him. "We'll do it the President's way. I'll order an e-vac. You can remote-detonate."

"You still don't think this will work," Kimsey said.

"What I know . . . is irrelevant," Truman admitted.

"We can't get online—you better get bomb status from the crew now," Kimsey advised him.

Grace stepped between Truman and the comm console. "Can they still take off?" she wanted to know.

"We hope so," Truman said. "We can't know if—"

POW! Grace slugged him across the face.

"That's my family up there, do you understand that?" she shrieked. She grabbed Truman's shirt in her fists.

"You pulled them into this! So I don't want to hear 'we hope so!'"

Truman held her by the shoulders, saw tears come to her eyes. "I'm feeling the same thing you are. . . ."

"No. No, you are not. You couldn't," she sobbed.

"And I'm sorry," Truman continued. "But it's not your family. It's everyone. Everyone's family. Can they still take off? I pray they can."

He waited for her to look him in the eye.

"Even more," he said, "I pray there'll be a place they can come home to."

———————————

Watts was using what strength she had left to prep for takeoff. She radioed a brief to Houston, "Electrical's unsteady but we have pre-launch phase two complete. . . ."

Outside, Harry watched Sharp and Gruber reassemble the nuke. Chick moved over to have a word.

"It's been twenty years with you, Harry," he said. "Every time I thought we couldn't do it, you proved me wrong. I admire that more than you think. Damn it, Harry"——Chick's voice cracked——"this time I was right."

Just then headlights washed across them. The second Armadillo had arrived!

Watts spotted it from the orbiter, too. "Houston!" she radioed. "You're not gonna believe this! The Armadillo! The other Armadillo! It's here!"

Watts didn't have to hear them to know that Mission Control was probably going wild.

The Armadillo came to a stop at the drilling hole. A. J. rose from the roof hatch.

"There's a great little Italian place like two miles that way!" he told them.

Harry shook his head and—yes—smiled.

"Ya feel like helping us drill a hole?" he wondered.

A. J. tightened, remembering the crash. "I've only got Bear and the cosmonaut. The others didn't make it," he said grimly.

Harry said, "We'll take all the help we can get."

A. J. nodded. "Then let's get dirty."

Watts gave Mission Control the news. "Drilling has recommenced, Houston."

Two hundred and fifty feet to go.

In one hour.

————

A. J. worked the control levers on the platform of the Armadillo feverishly, sending the tongs after pipe, working the drill, following Harry's orders from the site.

The asteroid sent them some recoil.

"Getting some kick!" Harry yelled. "Slow it down!"

"I'm drilling through her!" A. J. told him.

"No!"

"Harry," A. J. insisted, "if you're ever gonna trust me, do it now! We can't pull back! The bit'll get lodged, and the whole thing'll blow!"

Harry didn't think so. "The arm can't take the pressure!" he argued.

"You built her," A. J. told him. "Let me ride her! You've gotta trust me! If the bit gets chewed, we'll replace it! If the tranny blows, we'll throw on another one!"

"I've got some news for ya! We're all out of bits and trannies!"

That knocked the wind out A. J. "Oh...oh, shit."

The ground shook.

"A. J.!" Harry barked. "All right, I'm trusting you on this!"

"Now, wait a minute!" A. J. said back.

"No, kid, this is on your shoulders! Do it! *Punch it!*" Harry ordered.

"Shit..." A. J. groaned, throwing the drive switch.

The bit chewed into the rock, then dug like a mole to eight hundred feet. Harry was ecstatic.

"A. J.! *You tapped us a fault!*" he hooted. "Let's start pulling pipe!"

Now all they needed was a bomb.

Gruber and Sharp were putting the final touches on the hardware inside the nuke. As soon as the hole was clear, they were ready to drop her in for the big party.

A. J. put the arm in full-speed reverse, beating a retreat out of the shaft with Harry and Bear snapping off sections of pipe as they rose to the surface.

Then Bear slipped and dropped his wrench into the machinery.

Six thousand rpm's.

The engine ground horribly, jammed the drive, reversed, and hammered pipe back into the hole.

Harry, A. J., and the rest of the population on Earth had a plumbing problem. Fifty feet below the surface of the asteroid with thirty-eight minutes to fix the problem and go.

Watts got to be the one to give them the story back home. "Sir," she radioed, "there's been an accident. . . ."

———

Harry had an idea.

"Run me out some cable," he told A. J.

"You're not going down there," A. J. said.

"And *who* says?" Harry started running cable himself.

"I'm a better climber than you," A. J. said, "and I don't know how many decades younger."

"Back home I'd kick your ass for that."

"The truth hurts," A. J. said. "If we had more time, I'd say go for it."

Harry gave him a look, and then handed A. J. the cable.

"Hey," A. J. said, stepping to the shaft. "The bride's father usually pays for the wedding, right?"

Harry frowned. "You'd better start climbing," he growled.

———————

A. J. went down carrying a handheld cutter and a length of nylon line. At the obstruction, he cut eyes to run the line through.

Deep in its gut, the asteroid rumbled.

"Move fast, A. J.," Harry cautioned.

A. J. ran the line into the heart of the obstruction and tied it off for the winch.

The rumbling was mounting into a certified quake. A. J. shimmied up the pipe, praying against its collapse—

A geyser of methane gas plumed two hundred feet into the sky from the fault line splitting their way across the valley—then another—then another. An immense surge of gas engorged the fault line and inflated the shaft, blowing A. J. out like a cork out of a pop gun.

Harry grabbed the cable just in time.

"This thing definitely does not like us," Harry decided.

Chick agreed. "It knows we're here to kill it."

The quake along the fault line had created a boulder field of active rubble, Volkswagen-sized rocks bounding around like thundering tumbleweeds. Harry lashed A. J.'s safety line to the Armadillo, tying him off like a kid's balloon, while Sharp scrambled up the side to the multi-barrel phalanx cannon.

At that moment, another natural gas geyser bloomed a giant fireball from a fissure by the drilling hole, ramming Gruber with a wall of heat, slamming him into the Armadillo, killing him instantly.

Sharp unleashed a burst of cannon fire at the boulder field but there were too many of them. Now they knew what it felt like to be a billiard ball at the break.

One of the rollers ran over the grappling hook at the end of A. J.'s tether and gave him a jerk, then followed the line like a train on a track, flattening it and bringing A. J. down for a steamroller finish.

Sharp spotted him and dropped into the Armadillo, throwing it in drive and ramming the boulder off course at the last second.

Close, but no cigar. . . . The grappling hook was still deep in the boulder, and the runaway rock dragged A. J. flying and banging over the rubble. He'd seen surface trolling for swordfish behind a powerboat—this was what it was like to be the bait.

Somehow he managed to deploy the harness release and tumble off in time to see the mother of all bowling balls roll a spare directly over Harry and Chick.

Then it stopped.

A. J. didn't want to look at what kind of spot Harry and Chick had left, but he couldn't help it. There it was——

——They were alive! A shallow foxhole depression

in the surface had saved them. They got to their feet shakily and stumbled toward the Armadillo.

"We lost Gruber," Sharp said sadly.

Harry stopped at the hole. It was clear.

"Get the bomb," he said.

In *Freedom*, Watts had the ship ready for takeoff. Lev went to a window, looking for the rest of the team. The lights in the spacecraft came up momentarily then browned out.

"No . . . God, not now——" Watts moaned.

Lev turned. "Is this serious problem?"

———————

Sharp did final prep on the nuke with Harry and A. J. looking on. The last step was the button sequence to activate the countdown timer——he punched the code and——

——Nothing.

"What's wrong *now?*" Harry demanded. A. J. wasn't sure if he was talking to Sharp or to the bomb.

Sharp answered, horrified. "The timer, the remote, the whole thing——is dead."

"The bomb's no good?" A. J. heard himself babble.

"The trigger's dead." Sharp cursed. "Something must've fried when we took it apart."

About this Harry gave not one shit. "Sharp," he insisted, "how do we detonate this thing?"

"Now?" Sharp said. "Now the only way is manually."

A. J. asked for clarification: "You mean, *manually* manually?"

Harry sighed. "He means one of us has to stay."

———   ———

The buzz at Mission Control faded to the sound of a single chair squeaking and then total silence as Truman addressed the room.

"We're eighteen minutes from the Zero Barrier," he told them. "And we've got some bad news. The remote detonator on the bomb's been damaged...."

———   ———

The asteroid team was gathered in the orbiter.

"It takes two people to fly this thing," Sharp was saying. "Or I'd gladly trade places with any of you guys."

Rockhound, duct-taped to a chair, mumbled, "Yeah, sure you would!" They'd finally had to restrain him.

Sharp ignored him. "Either we all stay and die, or you guys draw straws," he said.

"We don't need to pick straws," Harry said. "I'll do it."

"Bullshit!" Lev spat. "I will let you volunteer for this so I can return to my country as the man who did not volunteer?"

Bear cut him off. "I'm the guy for the job. Besides

my bike, I've barely got anything back home anyway."

Rockhound chimed in. "You all might think I'm crazy now, but I'd really like this responsibility."

Harry shrugged. "Let's draw—do it quick."

Sharp nodded and presented them with a fisted bundle of electrical wires. "We'll go clockwise," he told them, giving Chick first draw.

"I'm not drawing against you, Harry," Chick argued.

"Goddamn it," Harry urged, "*I'm* drawing against *you!* Now *do it!*"

Chick drew a wire.

Then Lev. They looked about equal.

"Is this good or bad?" Lev wondered. They didn't play this where he was from.

Then A. J., whose wire appeared shorter. Then Harry, then Bear.

A. J.'s *was* shorter. "Oh, man . . ." he griped.

Harry cut in. "A. J., listen—"

"It's settled," A. J. said. "I'm the guy who gets to save the Earth." He checked his watch. "We've got eight minutes. Let's get it over with."

Sharp showed him the detonator. "You'll plug this into the port, press this trigger button. That's it."

A. J. nodded. Dead man walking.

———————

Alone together, Harry and A. J. left the airlock to walk the last steps from *Freedom* to the bomb.

A. J. held the detonator with resignation. "Do me a favor," he struggled to ask Harry, "and tell Grace——"

"No," Harry said.

A. J. couldn't believe they weren't any closer than that. Not after all they'd gone through.

"Harry, please," A. J. said, almost crying.

No.

Harry grabbed the mission patch on his spacesuit sleeve, ripped it off, and shoved it into A. J.'s suit pocket.

"Give that to Truman," he commanded. Then he yanked A. J.'s air tubes, choking off his breath instantly, stabbed the air-locked door, and grabbed the detonator.

"*This time it's my turn,*" he let A. J. know.

A. J. thrashed, gasping for air, as Harry pushed him into the elevator and slammed the door.

Locked inside, A. J. beat on the door.

"*Bullshit! This is my job!*" he bellowed.

Harry stood quietly at the port. "Go take care of my little girl," he told A. J. "That's your job. Go be the husband Grace deserves."

A. J. was furious. "I'm gonna get another suit!"

Harry showed his head. "Before, when I said you turned out to be a disappointment..." he said, then paused.

He smiled. "I meant it."

Their eyes locked. A. J. knew what Harry really

meant. Harry reached out his hand . . . and pushed the button that sent A. J. away.

When the elevator doors opened and A. J. fell out, Chick knew immediately what Harry'd done.

"That stubborn, iron-ass bastard," he said with great affection.

To the drilling hole, through a windstorm of ice and fine debris blowing off the leading edge of the asteroid, Harry walked alone.

CHAPTER NINETEEN

"Is he calling? Can he get through?" Grace worried, wondering if her dad could call home.

"There's been a change in plan," Truman said quietly.

Harry's voice cut in over the radio. "—e there? . . . oing . . . ough? . . . ybe. Grace? . . . an you hear me?"

A tech handed Grace a mike and stepped aside.

She stared at the static-filled monitor. Harry's face faded in and out—but she saw an expression. A look that was strained and tired.

She forced a smile.

"Dad," she started to say, then the tears welled up.

"I know I promised I was coming home," Harry told her, "but Grace, I've gotta break that promise."

Grace denied it. "Why can't they—?"

"Honey, stop," Harry said. "Listen to me. There isn't much time. I just want to tell you . . . I lied to you. When I said I was going along because I don't trust anyone else . . . that wasn't true."

The picture flashed out and back in.

". . . here because I love you," he said. Trying not to cry.

"I lied to you," Grace said back. "Okay? When I told you I didn't want to be like you? I am like you. We're two peas in a pod. Everything good I got from you, and I need you to know that. 'Cause right now I'm so scared. . . ."

Harry got a glimpse of the Earth, hanging like a blue balloon in the night sky. "There won't be anything to be scared of soon . . . and don't be scared for me, sweetheart. I'll be just fine. It's so beautiful up here."

He paused a moment to reflect on the canopy of stars overhead, the brilliant white moon.

"A wise man once told me that God gives us children so that we can have roses in December. You gave me a whole gardenful, Grace. You really did. . . . I want you to take care of your husband. I wish I could walk you down the aisle . . . but I'll look in on you from time to time. I love you, Gracie. . . ."

And he pulled the video link, sending Grace's monitors to static. Her fingers touched the screen, her knees felt weak. . . .

Watts's voice squawked a bland report over the radio: "O-2 vents closed, pressure loaded."

Then Sharp: "Engine board is green."

Harry's voice, transmitting from near the hole: "You've got two minutes, Sharp. I'm not waiting."

A moment of silence. Then Sharp: "Initiate thrusters."

Clark, from Houston: "*Freedom,* looking tight for ignition. . . ."

———————   ———————

Fuel valves! Watts thought. Frantic, she unstrapped herself from the chair and scrambled toward the cargo bay.

Fuel valves!

She dived into the service hatch and frantically worked the valves.

Lev appeared at her shoulder. "Is sticking, yes?"

"Back off!" Watts yelled. "You don't know the component!"

Sharp punched the thruster switch over and over. No response.

———————   ———————

Harry's voice: "What the hell are you doing in there? Get off this rock!"

No answer.

Harry: "Don't think I won't press this button!"

———————

Watts was going crazy trying to open the valves.

"Move away!" Lev shouted.

"Back off!" Watts fired back.

"Shit part Russian is same as shit part American! I spend year and a half on Russian space station! This is how we fix everydamnthing!"

Lev jerked her out of the way and banged the equipment over and over with a wrench. BAM! BAM! BAM—

—VROOM! It fired!

Freedom lifted away and headed for home.

CHAPTER TWENTY

"It's just you and me, and now it's my turn," Harry told the rock.

A fireball of burning gas rose into the sky.

"Complain all you want."

He raised the detonator to press the button and—

—WHAM! Three geysers of gas blew under his feet and threw the detonator from his hand.

And knocked Harry into the hole.

Ass first, he thought, trying to jam himself in the tube and stop his descent.

Banging against the wall, he broke his air supply.

———

Clark on the radio: "*Freedom*. We're thirty seconds to Zero Barrier. Where's the detonation?"

Sharp: "Something's wrong. We've gotta go back."

Watts: "There is no going back! We won't have enough fuel to make it home!"

Sharp: "Something's wrong!"

A. J.: "Even if something's wrong, Harry won't quit. he doesn't know how."

——————— ———————

Harry ran, gasping for air, dived for the detonator. One last look at beautiful Earth. Hoped he wasn't dreaming. Hoped he wasn't really dead, back there in the hole. Pushed the button—

——————— ———————

"I won."

CHAPTER TWENTY-ONE

The blast rear-ended *Freedom* like a semi and threw her into a crazy somersault, shaking up her contents.

"Be a shame to die now!" Chick piped up.

"Speak for yourself!" Rockhound complained around a half-torn gag of duct tape. "You don't owe a hundred grand to a bad-ass Italian!"

Unfortunately for Rockhound, they were home free.

———

The orbiter re-entered the atmosphere and screamed through the air, glowing red from the heat. It made the standard powerless freefall—a landing technique that on any other aircraft would be considered an emergency procedure.

Dust chirped as the tires hit concrete, banging

down, bouncing and racing to the end of the runway, slowing, stopping—

They made it.

"Get me the hell outta this goddamned thing," Chick whooped.

"Guys," Sharp warned them, "stay in your seats until they tell us what to do—there's a lot of people out there. It's gonna be a madhouse, so just hang tight, okay?"

A. J. turned to the others. "It's times like these you've gotta ask yourself, what would Harry do?"

———————

The shuttle doors opened onto a huge crowd, cheering and chanting and roaring.

Lev seemed moved. "I wonder if my family could get citizenship here...."

"Buddy," Rockhound explained, "at this point your family could have their own *talk show* here."

———————

Grace broke away from the reception area, and A. J. spotted her. They both ran and fell into each other's arms. Kissing, crying.

"He was a great man, Grace," A. J. told her.

"I know he was," she told him through the tears.

Sharp's voice cut in. "Ms. Stamper?"

Grace and A. J. let go, and she turned to him.

"Colonel Roger Sharp, United States Air Force, ma'am," he said.

Then he gave her a crisp salute.

"Request permission to shake the hand of the daughter of the bravest man I've ever met."

Grace smiled. Her eyes were dry. She straightened herself and offered her hand.

Truman arrived. A. J. handed him Harry's mission patch. "Harry wanted you to have this," he said.

Truman's eyes were wet.

"Thank you," he said to A. J.

Then to Harry Stamper, looking up—

Thank you.